KN JN 96

CULTURES OF THE WORLD

PUERTO RICO

PATRICIA LEVY

MARSHALL CAVENDISH
New York • London • Sydney

Reference edition published 1995 by
Marshall Cavendish Corporation
2415 Jerusalem Avenue
P.O. Box 587
North Bellmore
New York 11710

© Times Editions Pte Ltd 1995

Originated and designed by
Times Books International, an imprint of
Times Editions Pte Ltd

Printed in Singapore

Library of Congress Cataloging-in-Publication Data:
Levy, Patricia Marjorie.
    Puerto Rico / Patricia Levy.
        p. cm.—(Cultures Of The World)
    Includes bibliographical references and index.
    ISBN 1-85435-690-9 (set). — ISBN 1-85435-692-5 :
        1. Puerto Rico—Juvenile literature. [1. Puerto Rico.]
I. Title. II. Series.
F1958.3.L48 1994
972.95—dc20   94–22573
                       CIP
                       AC

Cultures of the World

Editorial Director	Shirley Hew
Managing Editor	Shova Loh
Editors	Elizabeth Berg
	Jacquiline King
	Dinah Lee
	Azra Moiz
	Sue Sismondo
Picture Editor	Susan Jane Manuel
Production	Anthony Chua
Design	Tuck Loong
	Ronn Yeo
	Felicia Wong
	Loo Chuan Ming
Illustrators	Anuar
	Chow Kok Keong
	William Sim
MCC Editorial Director	Evelyn M. Fazio
MCC Production Manager	Janet Castiglioni

INTRODUCTION

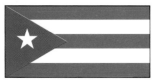

FOR CENTURIES, THE TINY ISLAND of Puerto Rico, with its few natural resources but great beauty, was the gateway to the whole Caribbean—whoever controlled Puerto Rico controlled the fabulous wealth of silver, gold, and cash crop fortunes in the region. With its unique Indian, African, and Spanish heritage, the spirit of Puerto Rico has expressed itself in many cultural traditions. Its people have taken their culture to the United States and permanently affected their new homeland with their vibrant lifestyles.

Today, the commonwealth of Puerto Rico stands at a crossroads, facing the decision of whether to merge its politics, economy, and culture with the United States, or to become an independent state and allow its fragile economy to support its young society. This book, one in the *Cultures of the World* series, studies the history of this country, its rich heritage and culture, and the many aspects of life that make this country so vibrant.

CONTENTS

Rock art—a young boy displays painted stones for tourists.

CONTENTS

Strolling guitar players entertain in a street band.

GEOGRAPHY

THE ISLAND OF PUERTO RICO lies at the northeastern edge of the Caribbean Sea, 1,000 miles southeast of Miami, Florida. Its closest neighbor to the west is the Dominican Republic, while the Virgin Islands lie to the east of Puerto Rico.

A rectangular shaped island of 3,435 square miles, Puerto Rico is about the same size as the state of Connecticut. The main island of Puerto Rico runs 111 miles from east to west and is 36 miles wide from north to south. It is also made up of three offshore islands—Vieques and Culebra on the east coast, and Mona on the west.

To the north of the main island are the relatively cold waters of the Atlantic Ocean, while its eastern and southern shores are warmed by the Caribbean Sea.

A CHAIN OF ISLANDS

Puerto Rico is part of a long cluster of islands in the Caribbean Sea called the Antilles. It is one of the smaller islands in the Greater Antilles—Cuba, Jamaica, and the island of Hispaniola, which includes Haiti and the Dominican Republic, are larger islands. This region is also known as the West Indies. East of Puerto Rico, the Virgin Islands and another chain of smaller islands make up the Lesser Antilles.

Puerto Rico is part of a chain of submerged extinct volcanoes that forms a shallow shelf around the island. But moving just two miles off the north shore, the sea floor plunges to 6,000 feet. The Puerto Rico Trench 45 miles to the north has even deeper sea depths—the 28,000 feet Milwaukee Deep is one of the world's deepest underwater chasms.

Opposite: **El Yunque National Forest in the Luquillo mountains.**

Below: **Puerto Rico has more than 300 miles of sandy beaches and rocky coastline, washed by the rough Atlantic Ocean to the north and the calm Caribbean Sea to the south.**

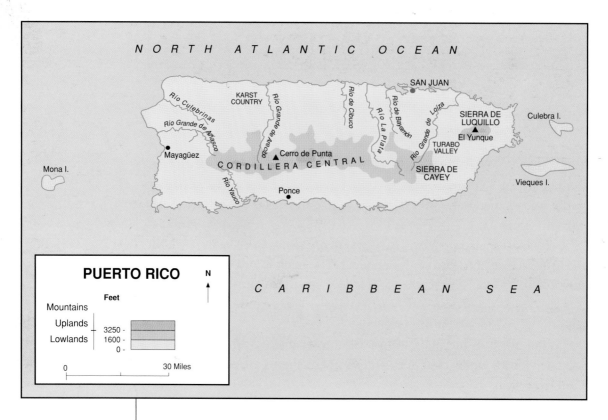

The map labels, reading across:

NORTH ATLANTIC OCEAN

SAN JUAN
KARST COUNTRY
Río Culebrinas
Río Grande de Arecibo
Río Grande de Añasco
Río de Cibuco
Río La Plata
Río de Bayamón
Río Grande de Loíza
SIERRA DE LUQUILLO
Culebra I.
El Yunque
TURABO VALLEY
Mayagüez
Cerro de Punta
CORDILLERA CENTRAL
SIERRA DE CAYEY
Mona I.
Río Yauco
Ponce
Vieques I.

CARIBBEAN SEA

PUERTO RICO   N

Feet

Mountains
Uplands
Lowlands

3250 -
1600 -
0 -

0   30 Miles

LAND REGIONS

For a small island, Puerto Rico has an amazing variety of physical features. Its mountainous interior is bounded by rolling foothills and flat coastal plains. Large areas are covered by rainforest, while on the southern side of the island, dry deserts and cacti can be found.

MOUNTAIN REGIONS The two main mountain ranges are the Cordillera Central and the Sierra de Luquillo. The Cordillera Central is the broadest and longest mountain range, stretching 60 miles from east to west with peaks over 3,000 feet high. Puerto Rico's highest mountain, the Cerro de Punta (4,389 feet), is found here.

A lower but more well known peak is the 3,483 feet El Yunque (meaning "the anvil") in the Luquillo mountains in the east. This area is now a nature reserve. A smaller mountain range, the Sierra de Cayey, is in the southeast of the island.

THE COASTAL PLAINS The northern coastal plain of the island is a narrow strip of land five miles wide and 100 miles long. It holds the bulk of Puerto Rico's population and most of its major industries. In the past, this area was fertile farming land where sugarcane and pineapples were grown. But this has since given way to urban and industrial development, with high-rise apartments, tourist hotels, and factories.

The eastern coastal plain is less densely populated but is a growing tourist area with good beaches. Some farming is still done there. The area has one of the world's largest naval bases, fueling United States ships in the area. The east coast is a traditional tobacco growing area.

The western coastal plain is still agricultural, growing sugarcane, fruits, and vegetables. Coffee plantations are found in the hill country inland.

The southern coastal plain is the newest tourist center in Puerto Rico. Traveling along a new highway from the capital San Juan in the north to Ponce on the south coast now takes an hour. Some of this area is still agricultural land—the semiarid land is excellent for growing sugarcane.

A small town set in the foothills of the Cordillera Central. As most mountain areas are too rocky and steep for cultivation, they have been protected from exploitation. Many still are covered in primary rainforest untouched by humans. The surrounding foothills, however, have been cultivated for agriculture.

Karst country. Rain seeping through porous limestone has carved huge caves and long underground passages in this region.

Inland from the southern coastal plain lie the foothills of the Cordillera Central. This southern hill region grows coffee, corn, and beans.

THE TURABO VALLEY Running west from the east coast into the central mountain range is the Turabo Valley. It is formed by the meeting of three mountain ranges—the Luquillo to the north and east, the Cayey to the south, and the Cordillera Central to the west. At the farthest point in the valley lies Caguas, Puerto Rico's largest inland city. Puerto Rico's only navigable river, the Río Grande de Loíza, flows through the Turabo Valley.

This area is mainly agricultural land. The town of Loíza sits at the northwestern end of the valley, separated from San Juan to the north by dense mangrove swamps. It is home to many people of African descent who came here as slaves and then settled after slavery was abolished.

KARST COUNTRY In the northwest of the island in the Arecibo region is a very unusual geological feature known as karst.

One of the oldest rock formations in the world, a karst terrain is formed as rainfall gradually erodes limestone rocks along joints and cracks. Since limestone is very soluble in rainwater, tunnels and caves are formed below the rock surface over the years. Eventually, all surface water disappears into underground tunnels, leaving unusual hillocks called *mogotes* ("moh-GOH-tehs," meaning miniature hills) that are around 200 to 300 feet high.

The karst region is covered in forest and scrub, making hiking in the area quite dangerous because of concealed sinkholes (holes formed when soluble rock is eroded). It is also famous for having the Arecibo Observatory, which houses the world's largest radio-telescope in a hollow basin formed by *mogotes*. The radio-telescope measures 1,320 feet in diameter and has a surface area of 40 acres.

THE OFFSHORE ISLANDS The largest island is Vieques, nine miles east of Puerto Rico. A large part of its 51.5 square miles is used by the United States Navy's Atlantic Fleet Weapons Training Facility. It has a small mountain range, some primary rainforest, and wildlife, including wild ponies descended from those bred by the Spanish settlers in the 16th century. The island's population is around 8,000. Most of the land is owned by the U.S. Navy, although some farming still goes on, mainly of sugarcane.

Farther east is the Culebra archipelago, which consists of a main island and 20 surrounding coral islets. The main island is flatter than Vieques and has a few streams and a semiarid climate. About 2,000 people live on it, mainly engaged in subsistence agriculture. Most of the islets form a wildlife preserve for birds and turtles.

Mona Island is 42 miles southwest of the mainland and is 20 square miles in size. It was once a lookout point for pirates but is now a wildlife sanctuary with a semiarid landscape.

The islet of Caja de Muertos (meaning "dead man's coffin") lies 13 miles off the coast of Ponce. It is a nature reserve sheltering endangered plants and animals typical of the dry subtropical climate.

Puerto Rico's offshore islands attract tourists and nature lovers.

Although Puerto Rico is very mountainous, it has few large rivers because its landmass is so small.

CLIMATE

Puerto Rico is situated in the tropical zone, but the high temperatures and humidity are moderated by the tradewinds, steady easterly winds that blow toward the equator.

Average temperatures range between 70° and 80° Fahrenheit, although some regions have more extreme temperatures. The weather is pleasant and cool in the mountains and on the coast, but can be uncomfortably hot farther inland. In summer on the south coast, the temperature can be as high as 100°F. It has also fallen to 39°F in the mountains in winter. In the Cordillera Central, the temperature drops one degree for every 500 feet in altitude. December to March are the cooler months.

Rainfall is fairly even throughout the year, although May to September are wetter months. Rainfall varies from 29 inches in the dry south to 108 inches in the mountains, and 180 inches around El Yunque. Parts of Puerto Rico are often flooded due to the high rainfall.

HURRICANE FORECASTING

As the Caribbean has the world's third highest number of hurricanes per year, forecasting when hurricanes will occur is extremely important. In modern times Puerto Ricans are given advance warning of impending hurricanes. People listen to public service warnings and plot the path of the storm on maps printed specially by local businesses. But in Puerto Rico there is also an interesting folk superstition that when the avocado harvest is good, the country will be protected from hurricanes.

This was put to the test in 1969 when hurricane Camille looked like it was about to hit the island. Avocado farmers assured the people they would be safe because the avocados were good that year. Strangely, the farmers were right and the hurricane veered away at the last moment. But just for added protection, many households keep a statue of the Virgin Mary and place jars containing "holy water" (water blessed by a priest) around the house to keep the hurricanes at bay.

June to December is a worrying time for Puerto Ricans as this is the hurricane season. Ever since records began to be kept in 1508, Puerto Rico has experienced 73 hurricanes. The most serious ones in living memory hit Puerto Rico in 1928 and 1932, when many people were killed and millions of dollars of crops and property were damaged. The most recent hurricane to hit Puerto Rico was Hurricane Hugo in 1989, which luckily did not cause a great deal of damage. Other hurricanes have also passed close by the island but left it undamaged.

RIVERS AND LAKES

The strongest rivers flow from the Cordillera Central to the north coast. The Río La Plata is the longest river at 46 miles, with its source in the Cayey mountains. The Río Grande de Loíza is the widest river and has its source in the southeast. It is well known, especially since it is the only navigable river in Puerto Rico.

Puerto Rico also has several man-made lakes formed by damming rivers. These provide the power for hydroelectric plants, which in the past produced most of Puerto Rico's electricity. The lakes are mostly set high up in the mountains. Many have been stocked with fish and provide recreation areas for tourists and Puerto Ricans.

Although the Caribbean lies in an active earthquake region, there have been no major earthquakes in Puerto Rico since the early years of the 20th century.

MAJOR CITIES

The population is increasing and more land is being used for tourist developments, with the result that many smaller towns are beginning to link together into suburbs of the bigger cities. As the two major cities, Ponce and San Juan, are only an hour's drive apart, some people live in one city and commute to the other.

SAN JUAN Puerto Rico's oldest city and its capital, San Juan, was founded in 1519 by Spanish settlers. Its population today stands at almost one million. Part of the city is built on an island linked to the north coast of

San Juan is a picturesque mixture of old and new, with classical Spanish architecture in the old parts of the city and modern steel and glass buildings in the business district of Santurce.

Puerto Rico by a bridge. Its streets are iron paved, and its houses are brightly painted.

San Juan is the industrial, economic, and intellectual heart of the island, with several universities, the main airport, and sugar, tobacco, and clothing industries. It is also a major tourist and banking center for many other Caribbean countries.

PONCE With a population of 400,000, Ponce is Puerto Rico's second largest as well as second oldest city. This major shipping port is located on the southern coast. It has an airfield and a major highway links it to San Juan. Its industries are canning, sugar, and iron. Ponce is also a major tourist attraction because of its many historical buildings. The city is situated in a "rain shadow" where afternoon storms are blocked by the Cordillera Central, so Ponce enjoys brilliant sunny weather for most of the year. It is known to its inhabitants as "the pearl of the south."

Fajardo is a sugarcane center and port on the east coast. Boats leave from here to go to Vieques and Culebra islands.

MAYAGUEZ The smallest of Puerto Rico's three major cities, Mayagüez is situated on the west coast. It was established more recently and has a high population of North American expatriates. Its major industry, fish packing, provides over 60% of the tuna eaten in the United States. Many pharmaceutical industries are also located here. The University of Puerto Rico's agricultural college is located here, close to the United States Department of Agriculture's Tropical Research Station, which has one of the largest collections of tropical and subtropical plants in the world.

Although three-fourths of Puerto Rico was covered by forest a century ago, only 1% of its forests today are original primary forests, untouched by humans.

FLORA AND FAUNA

Considering its small size, Puerto Rico has an amazing diversity of plants and animals in its rainforests, semiarid deserts, and coral reefs.

El Yunque National Forest in the Luquillo mountains has the largest expanse of forest in Puerto Rico. Part of the United States Forest Service system and its only tropical rainforest, El Yunque has 240 species of trees, more than 200 types of fern, and at least 60 species of birds. The most well known animal specie is the *coquí* ("koh-KEE"), a small tree frog only one-and-a-half inches long that has a sweet, musical call. The Puerto Rican parrot, a rare creature, lives in the rainforest. Only one flock of this endangered species remains.

Because of its height, El Yunque has a wide range of vegetation. Below 2,000 feet grows the tabanuco forest, which is similar to rainforests in tropical America and is named for a common native tree. Higher up is the palo colorado forests or montane forest covered in mosses. (Montane forests are forests found at high altitudes.) Sierra palms farther up provide tropical cover for steep slopes. At the very top is dwarf forest, whose stunted condition is due to the thin soil on high peaks and ridges.

Elsewhere on the island, mangrove swamps with trees specially adapted to living underwater can be found. Their long, exposed roots provide a habitat for many animal species. On the northwest coast is subhumid forest, where satinwood trees and mahogany are becoming increasingly rare. The south coast with its semiarid climate has thorny dry forest areas with cactus and spiny plants, and trees such as the Caribbean silk cotton tree, which can live

The musical cry of the *coquí*, Puerto Rico's most famous animal, is often mistaken for that of a bird.

Vegetation in Puerto Rico ranges from cacti in the dry regions to flowers such as the brightly colored *flamboyan* ("flam-BOH-yahn") or poinciana.

for 300 years. Mona Island also has vegetation typical of semiarid regions, including the tiny barrel cactus and organ pipe cactus similar to those found in the Arizona desert. It is also home to enormous lizards and iguanas and the booby, a red-footed bird.

The nearly extinct *ausubo* ("ah-oo-SOO-boh"), a kind of ironwood tree, is found in Puerto Rico. The wood resists rot and termites, and was used in many early buildings to make roof beams. When older buildings are demolished, the Institute of Puerto Rican Culture salvages the beams and stores them for restoration projects.

Puerto Rico is also home to many exotic species of arthropods including 15-inch-long centipedes with a painful bite. Several species of spiders that look dangerous but are harmless live on the island, including the *araña boba* ("ah-RAH-nyah BOH-bah"), or silly spider, and the giant crab spider. The poisonous black widow spider is another resident.

Around the coasts are many beautiful coral reefs with fire corals and brain corals. These provide a home for 2,000 different species of fish, including striking orange and blue parrot fish, red striped groupers, butterfly fish, and the pufferfish, which swells up when threatened. Jellyfish are also common around the coasts of Puerto Rico—the locals call them *agua viva* ("AH-goo-ah VEE-vah," or living water).

Animals more commonly found in Puerto Rico are iguanas, guinea pigs, and mongooses. The most common bird is the *reinita* ("ray-in-EET-ah," meaning little queen), which is very tame and often raids kitchens for morsels of food.

HISTORY

FOR CENTURIES, PUERTO RICO'S history has been bound up with the powers that colonized it. From the 15th to the 19th century, Spain was its colonial master, after which ownership of the island was transferred to the United States.

Ever since then, much of Puerto Rico's history has focused on its political status—whether it should become independent, remain part of the United States commonwealth, or become the 51st state of the union.

EARLY HISTORY

The earliest known inhabitants of Puerto Rico were the Ciboney who migrated to the island on primitive rafts from Florida via Cuba. They were hunter-gatherers, living on wild fruits and roots, and fishing for survival. Remains of their culture have been found close to beaches, but as no arrowheads have been found, they probably did not use iron or other metals. The Ciboney were followed by the Igneri who came around 200 B.C. from Venezuela. These people also left traces of their culture through their multicolored pottery.

The Igneri were later replaced around A.D. 1000 by the Taíno, whose name means "gentle." The Taíno were not primitive people. They were skilled engineers and sailors who traded with other civilizations in South and Central America. They also farmed the land, growing cotton, corn, tobacco, cassava, and sweet potatoes. They had no domesticated animals except mute dogs, and their meat supply came from birds and poultry.

Although the Taíno were peaceful people, they were continually at war with an aggressive neighboring tribe called the Carib, which had nearly destroyed other Taíno Indians in the Lesser Antilles. By the end of the 15th century, it seemed that the Carib would also wipe out the Taíno from Boriquén.

Called Boriquén (meaning Land of the Noble Lord) by the native Taíno Indians, the island was renamed San Juan Bautista by Christopher Columbus in 1493. However, after 1521, the island came to be known as Puerto Rico, meaning "rich port," and its capital city was called San Juan.

Opposite: **A statue of Christopher Columbus on a pedestal in the Plaza de Colón, San Juan's main square. The statue was erected in 1893 to mark the 400th anniversary of Columbus's arrival in Puerto Rico.**

In less than 100 years, Spanish rule in Puerto Rico completely wiped out the native Taíno population. From 53,000 Taínos who lived on the island when it was discovered by Columbus, the population shrank to only a few thousand in the 1530s. In 1582, the governor reported to Spain that the Taíno Indian population was virtually nil.

THE SPANISH ARRIVAL

Puerto Rico was discovered by Christopher Columbus when he made his second journey to the Caribbean in 1493 in search of Hispaniola. Naming the island San Juan Bautista after the heir to the Spanish throne, he claimed it for Spain. But it was not until 1508 that the first Spanish settlers, led by Juan Ponce de León, established a settlement there. The local Taíno welcomed the settlers, helping them to find a suitable spot to build a settlement. This was named Caparra and was situated on the north shore of the island, but was shifted in 1519 to the present location of San Juan.

The Spaniards' main interest in the island was to obtain gold. At first the Taíno innocently exchanged gold jewelry for cheap trinkets offered by the Spanish. When they realized what a poor exchange this was, they became reluctant to show the Spaniards the source of their gold or to help excavate it. The Spaniards then introduced a system of labor called *repartimiento* ("reh-part-im-YEN-toh") that forced the Taíno to work for them in exchange for protection and Christianity. It was just like slavery, with the Indians forced to work in gold mines and on plantations that the Spaniards cultivated.

Eventually, the Taíno were totally crushed by Spanish rule. Their religion was suppressed by Catholic priests accompanying the Spanish settlers, and they were forced to wear clothes for the first time. Many Taínos committed suicide and killed their own children rather than live in slavery. The Spaniards also brought European diseases to which the Taíno had not developed resistance, so many died from disease. Rebellions broke out in 1511, 1513, and 1518, all of which were crushed by Spain. More Taíno fled the island, joined the aggressive Carib, and began raiding coastal settlements in Puerto Rico. The raids and rebellions became so serious that a fortress was built in San Juan for protection.

A PERIOD OF DECLINE

In the early years, Puerto Rico was a profitable Spanish colony mining gold and producing cash crops. But by the 1530s, gold mines were exhausted, the Taíno had died or run away, and the settlements were under attack by French privateers, Taíno, and Carib. As Spanish settlers began leaving the island, the governor banned all Spaniards from leaving. To set an example, he publicly cut off the legs of two men who tried to leave. To replace the Taíno who were dying out, African slaves were imported to do the manual labor. By 1530, half the population of 3,000 consisted of slaves.

By the 17th century, Spanish power in the Caribbean had declined. The French, Dutch, and English gained more control, and took over Jamaica and some of the Lesser Antilles. Although Puerto Rican landowners and ranchers were required to sell their goods only to Spain, they began trading illegally with the enemies of Spain. An illegal trade in hides and sugar developed, particularly around Ponce on the south coast. English, French, and Dutch traders openly traded goods, often with the Spanish officials who were supposed to keep these traders off the island.

The fortress of San Felipe del Morro (called El Morro) was begun in 1539 to ward off attacks from the sea. It was the strongest Spanish fortress in the Caribbean, with 18-foot-thick walls rising 140 feet above the sea. Another fort, San Cristóbal, was built between 1631 and 1771 to protect San Juan from land invasions.

GATEWAY TO THE INDIES

For centuries, Puerto Rico was the Spanish gateway to the West Indies, as tradewinds blowing southwest guided sailing ships into the heart of the Caribbean.

In the 15th century, Spain had control of large parts of the Caribbean and South America. As the British, Dutch, and French also began to establish a presence, Puerto Rico's strategic importance became evident. In the 16th century, Spanish fleets carrying valuable cargoes of Mexican and Peruvian silver were under constant attack by English and French privateers.

The French, English, and Dutch made many attempts to capture Puerto Rico in the 16th and 17th centuries. French privateers attacked the island in 1528 and 1538. In 1596, the first major English attempt to take the island was repelled. In another attempt in 1599, the English fleet landed east of San Juan and attacked from inland, thus avoiding the strong fortifications built to repel invaders from the sea. San Juan was taken, but not for long. The Spanish besieged the city from guerrilla positions inland and were able to drive the English out when the latter were weakened by a dysentery epidemic. In 1625, the Dutch captured San Juan in the same way as the British, but before disease and starvation drove the Dutch out, they burned most of the city to the ground.

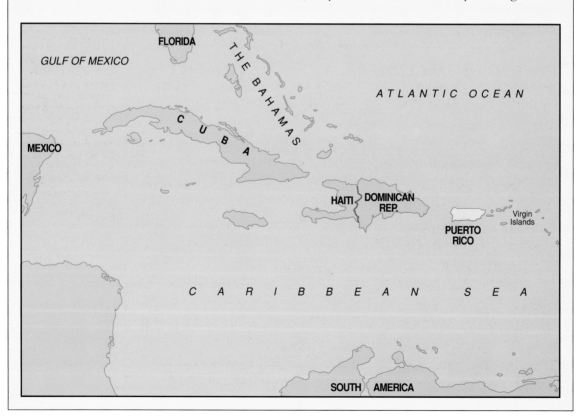

ECONOMIC RECOVERY

In 1765, Alejandro O'Reilly, an Irishman employed by the Spanish king, arrived in Puerto Rico to take stock of the island and assess its fortifications. He was dismayed by what he found. The troops were ill-equipped, badly paid, and undisciplined, while the fortifications were in a bad state of repair. Puerto Ricans were the poorest people in the Americas. There were no roads, few schools, little sanitation, and illegal trade still flourished with the English and French. The population of the island was at a critical level—of the total population of 44,000, there were only several hundred Spaniards, 5,000 slaves, and the rest were racially mixed people.

O'Reilly's recommendations to solve the problems brought recovery to Puerto Rico. By the end of the 18th century, the population had tripled to 155,000, mostly due to Spanish immigrants taking up offers of free land. The increased population size made it profitable for trading ships to call at Puerto Rican ports. Military strength increased, and the island was also better defended in 1797 when another English invasion was repelled. Between 1750 and 1800, 18 new towns were established.

Trade between the colonies and Spain was encouraged. Sugar, cotton, tobacco, and coffee plantations were improved by investment in machinery and better trade agreements.

Sugarcane was brought to the Caribbean by Christopher Columbus in 1493 and was first planted in Puerto Rico in 1515. Puerto Rico's sugar industry received a major boost in 1789 when French plantation owners fleeing a slave revolt on San Domingo came to Puerto Rico and set up new plantations on the island. Since then, the sugar industry has remained an important part of Puerto Rico's economy.

A mural in Christopher Columbus Park near the town of Aguada showing working conditions under slavery.

EARLY NATIONALISM

By the early 19th century, Spain's control over its colonies had weakened. There were rebellions in Mexico, Venezuela, Colombia, and other areas, until all that remained of the Spanish empire was Puerto Rico and Cuba. This benefited the colony, which was once again able to trade with other countries in 1815. For the first time American trading ships became a common sight in Puerto Rican harbors. Puerto Rico traded sugar, molasses, rum, coffee, and tobacco in exchange for American wheat, pork, and manufactured goods.

By this time, most of the wealth lay in the hands of Spanish landowners and administrators whose loyalties were to Spain. Although the mass of the population were racially mixed peasant workers, there was also a Creole elite, racially mixed families who had developed a sense of national identity. These people began to demand partial independence, new roads, schools, and an assembly of their own. Spain replied with trade concessions, reformed taxes, and greater incentives for foreign settlers. But no political autonomy was allowed.

In 1868, growing nationalism, a repressive government, and the refusal of the landowners to free their slaves erupted in open rebellion.

Ramón Emeterio Betances, a doctor who became a nationalist spokesman, called for independence. He was exiled from Puerto Rico, and in 1862, he issued his "Ten Commandments of Freedom," demanding the abolition of slavery and independence for the island. From exile in San Domingo he began planning a revolution. Although Betances was captured, his supporters decided to go ahead with the rebellion.

AN END TO SLAVERY

By the mid-19th century, Puerto Rico's economy depended heavily on African slavery. Worried about the effect of slave rebellions in other parts of the Caribbean, the Puerto Rican authorities took steps to prevent this happening on their island.

The Bando Negro decree of 1848 introduced the death penalty for any disobedient behavior by a slave, while any free African person showing resistance to a white man's wishes would have his right hand cut off. Just for being rude, a free African man could get five years in jail, and all African people from the Caribbean and the United States were banned from entering Puerto Rico. As a result of these cruel laws, many small rebellions took place and slaves ran away to the mountains.

In spite of pressure from other European countries, Spain kept delaying the abolition of slavery. Slavery was finally abolished in 1873. Even then, all slaves had to work for another three years and wait two years more before they gained full civil rights. When Puerto Rico's 30,000 slaves were finally set free, about half of them stayed as employees with the men who once had been their masters.

To deal with the dissatisfaction of the peasants and the middle-class Creoles, Governor Miguel de La Torre encouraged the islanders to have a good time. His administration became known as the regime of the three B's—botella, baile, baraja ("bot-ELL-yah, BUY-leh, bah-RAH-hah," meaning drinking, dancing, and gambling).

At midnight on September 23, 1868, Betances' supporters captured the town of Lares, arrested the mayor, and held a celebratory mass in the town's church. They declared a republic, named a president, and offered freedom to all slaves who joined them. They moved on to San Sebastian but were driven back, and in the guerilla warfare that followed, most rebels were killed or taken prisoner. Since then, this day is known as Grito de Lares, the day on which independence was first declared in Puerto Rico.

By 1897, the nationalist movement in Puerto Rico forced Spain to give Puerto Rico some autonomy. By the Charter of Autonomy 1897, Puerto Rico was allowed to send delegates to the Spanish legislature, elect a house of representatives, and take part in the administrative council. The governor was still appointed by Spain, although with fewer powers, and he nominated seven Senate members. In May 1898, after four centuries of Spanish rule, a new autonomous Puerto Rican government took office, led by Luis Muñoz Rivera.

THE SPANISH-AMERICAN WAR

On July 25, 1898, just a few weeks after Puerto Rico's new autonomous government took office, 16,000 United States troops led by General Nelson A. Miles invaded Puerto Rico and landed at Guánica Bay on its south coast.

Although San Juan was bombed and there were minor battles with Spanish troops, the Spanish-American War was over in Puerto Rico in 17 days. Yauco was taken, Ponce surrendered, Mayagüez fell, and then the Spanish surrendered. In December 1898, under the Treaty of Paris, Puerto Rico was handed over to the United States.

The locals were friendly—they knew America to be a rich, democratic nation and hoped for a better life under American rule. The liberal leaders who won autonomy from Spain only to lose it to the United States demanded a referendum, but they were ignored.

LUIS MUÑOZ RIVERA

An important figure in Puerto Rico's history, Luis Muñoz Rivera is regarded by many Puerto Ricans as "the George Washington of Puerto Rico." He was a liberal-minded journalist during the time when Puerto Rico was trying to claim autonomy from Spain.

He played an important role in negotiating the Charter of Autonomy with Spain and was a party to Puerto Rico's short-lived independence before the United States' invasion in 1898. Under American rule, he became Puerto Rico's representative in Washington and successfully campaigned for the establishment of United States citizenship for Puerto Ricans, as well as an elected Puerto Rican legislature.

AMERICAN RULE

Puerto Rico's political status under American rule was set out in the Foraker Act of 1900. Under this act, Puerto Ricans were neither United States citizens nor citizens of an independent nation. An assembly with a majority of Americans was set up whose laws were subject to veto by the U.S. Congress. The governor was appointed by the United States. Puerto Ricans ended up with even less control over their country than under autonomy from Spain.

Dislike of the Foraker Act grew so strong that the assembly refused to approve any legislation. The most important objection was the issue of citizenship. After many years of protests and negotiation, the Jones Act of 1916 finally gave United States citizenship to Puerto Ricans during World War I, when German warships were prowling around the Caribbean. Puerto Ricans could accept American citizenship or refuse it, in which case they lost many civil rights. As United States citizens, they could be drafted for military service and were still ruled by an American governor appointed by the U.S. president.

The 1930s were terrible years for Puerto Rico. Two hurricanes hit the island and the economic depression brought mass unemployment and starvation. Conditions became worse than under the worst excesses of Spanish rule. The independence movement grew more militant. Its leaders claimed that the United States' acquisition of the island was illegal since Puerto Rico had been an autonomous state at the time. Violence broke out in 1936 and 1937.

In 1943, the American governor of Puerto Rico, Rexford G. Tugwell, recommended that the U.S. Congress permit Puerto Ricans to elect their own governor. Finally, in 1946, President Harry Truman appointed Jesús T. Piñero as the first Puerto Rican governor of the island.

The island that the United States took over in 1898 had 900,000 people—a tiny upper-class elite, a Creole middle class, and a vast majority of illiterate and poor, living in wooden huts and eating one meal a day. There were hardly any surfaced roads and little property of any great value.

In 1947, the U.S. Congress enacted a bill allowing an elected governor for Puerto Rico. In the first election for governor held in 1948, Luis Muñoz Marín became the first elected Puerto Rican to hold this position.

On October 30, 1950, the Puerto Rico Commonwealth Bill was signed by President Truman in the United States, under which Puerto Rico became an American commonwealth with its own constitution. In June 1951, the people of Puerto Rico approved this arrangement and voted by nearly four to one to maintain the commonwealth relationship with the United States. However, the nationalist movement still remained active and campaigned for complete independence.

The Puerto Rican and United States flags are always flown together, symbolizing Puerto Rico's status as a commonwealth.

THE "NEW LIFE"

In 1968, Luis A. Ferré was elected governor and promised a new life for the people of Puerto Rico. His reforms gave salary increases to civil servants, cracked down on drug dealers, and set a minimum wage for farm workers. More importantly, he set about improving the sugarcane industry with new technology and set up birth control clinics all over the island.

Ferré's eventual aim was for Puerto Rico to become the 51st U.S. state. But this was opposed by those in favor of the existing association with the United States and by the independence movement. The opposition became increasingly militant to the idea of statehood, and in 1969, a crisis erupted after a Puerto Rican draftee refused to enter the U.S. Army. Student riots followed between pro-independence and pro-commonwealth protesters. Ten thousand people marched in a demonstration against the draft.

MODERN TIMES

During the 1970s, political dispute over Puerto Rico's status calmed down a little, although there were calls for another referendum to decide the issue. In the 1972 election, the pro-commonwealth party won the governorship, and then in 1976, the pro-statehood party won control.

Through most of the 1980s, Rafael Hernández Colón was in power as governor. In the 1992 election, he offered the nation a referendum on democratic rights that would have made possible an enhanced commonwealth status. This was rejected by the electorate. He chose to stand down as governor, and in 1992, Pedro Rosello was elected governor. His party favors statehood, so another referendum is planned, this time putting the question of statehood directly to the electorate.

A labor protest in San Juan. About 11% of the workforce is unionized.

GOVERNMENT

IN 1950, PUERTO RICO'S political status changed from being a United States protectorate or colony, to being part of the United States commonwealth. This made it a self-governing territory, although the United States still has some control over its internal affairs.

WHO GOVERNS?

The Commonwealth of Puerto Rico has a constitution similar to that of the United States. It has a democratically elected government with executive, legislative, and judicial branches.

Some aspects of Puerto Rico's government are handled by the federal government of the United States. The federal government manages all the island's foreign affairs and defense. It also manages some internal matters such as the post office, customs, and quarantine. The U.S. Federal Aviation

Opposite: **A police officer on beachside patrol.**

Left: **La Forteleza was the first Spanish fortress to be built in Puerto Rico, in 1533. It guarded the Bay of San Juan in the 16th century but is now the home of the governor of Puerto Rico. It is the oldest governor's mansion in use today in all the Americas.**

Although they are U.S. citizens, Puerto Ricans do not have the right to vote in U.S. presidential elections. Puerto Rico has one representative in the U.S. Congress, but this representative cannot vote on legislation before Congress. Puerto Ricans are eligible to serve in the U.S. armed forces, and have fought for the United States in four wars

Administration, the Federal Communications Commission, the Federal Housing Administration, and the Federal Bureau of Investigation operate on the island. These federal agencies employ many Puerto Ricans whose salaries are funded from Washington. In return, the United States gets benefits such as large areas of land for naval and military bases.

THE CONSTITUTION

The island has a written constitution similar to the United States, but with some differences. The death penalty and phone tapping are prohibited. Printing presses are safe from closure or confiscation by the state.

Discrimination on the grounds of race, color, sex, birth, social origins, or political or religious convictions is unconstitutional. The right to a minimum wage, an eight-hour working day, and special pay rates for overtime work are also part of the constitution. Collective bargaining, unions, and striking and picketing are all guaranteed by the constitution.

THE EXECUTIVE

The governor is head of the cabinet and is elected every four years. He must be a Puerto Rican, at least 35 years old, a U.S. citizen, and must also be a resident of the country. He is commander-in-chief of the National Guard, which is administered and funded by the U.S. government.

The governor chooses a cabinet of 10 department heads with the advice of the Senate. These departments are in charge of education, health, agriculture, commerce, finance, justice, labor, public works, state services, and social services. They are answerable only to the governor. Also reporting directly to the governor are executive agencies and public corporations, bodies such as the universities, the bus authority, and organizations for urban renewal.

THE LEGISLATURE

Puerto Rico has a bicameral legislature—a Senate and a House of Representatives. Twenty-seven members are elected to the Senate and 51 members to the House of Representatives. To guard against domination of the legislature by one party, the number of seats are increased if one party gains two-thirds or more of the seats. These new seats are given to the minority parties according to their support among the electorate.

Senators and representatives must be U.S. citizens at least 30 years old, must be able to write either Spanish or English, and must have lived in Puerto Rico for two years. Non-Puerto Ricans can also be senators or representatives provided they are U.S. citizens.

In reading through and passing laws, the legislature can overrule the governor's veto on a bill if it has been passed twice by a two-thirds majority. Most members have other occupations besides their responsibilities as legislators.

The Senate and House of Representatives meet at the Capitol building in San Juan.

The Customs House in San Juan harbor flies the United States and Puerto Rican flags. Customs matters in Puerto Rico are administered by the U.S. Customs Service.

THE JUDICIARY

Puerto Rico has a Supreme Court with nine judges and a chief justice. Below this are 9 high courts, 37 district courts, and 42 justices of the peace. Judges are appointed rather than elected. They cannot take part in any political activity and have some independence from the executive and legislative bodies. The outcome of a trial disputed in any of these courts will go to a higher court until it reaches the U.S. Supreme Court.

Since 1950, there has been an enormous increase in crime in Puerto Rico, particularly in drug-related crime. Mugging and burglary are more common. As a result, the courts are faced with a large backlog of people awaiting trial. The constitution guarantees that no one is kept in jail for longer than six months while waiting for trial.

POLITICAL PARTIES

The four main political parties in Puerto Rico have different views on the issue of the political status of the island.

The Partido Popular Democratico (PPD) is in favor of remaining a commonwealth of the United States, while the Partido Nuevo Progressivo (PNP) supports the idea of becoming the 51st state of the union. These two parties have dominated political life in Puerto Rico over the last 40 years.

The Partido Independista Puertorriqueño (PIP) favors complete independence. A fourth party, which is relatively new and has some support, is the Partido Socialista, a socialist organization.

Political banners outside the Capitol in San Juan.

COMMONWEALTH, UNION, OR INDEPENDENCE?

Discussion of Puerto Rico's political future is an emotional issue. It is so hotly debated that many cafés and shops put up notices asking customers not to "talk politics" on the premises.

Puerto Rico still has to make a decision on its status that has dominated its politics for over 90 years, but nowadays the decision seems to be one of economics rather than politics.

Commonwealth status has brought much revenue and foreign investment into Puerto Rico. American businesses have also benefited from tax allowances. Many people believe that if Puerto Rico lost its commonwealth status and became independent, much of this economic advantage would be lost as foreign and American businesses may then pull out in search of cheaper labor and better tax breaks. On the other hand, those advocating statehood say that joining the United States union would bring large amounts of welfare money to the poor of the island.

Nationalist supporters, however, believe that independence would not drive businesses away. Many firms have invested large amounts of money in training and plants in Puerto Rico, and they would be unlikely to pack up and move away, as this would mean higher costs. Also, if Puerto Rico were a U.S. state, its people would have to pay federal taxes. This would put a great burden on Puerto Ricans, who already pay high local taxes.

Another argument against joining the United States union is that, as the 51st state, Puerto Rico would be in danger of being the poorest state in the union, and of losing its culture as it is absorbed into the mainstream of American life. It also stands to lose its Spanish national language in place of English, which would be unacceptable to many Puerto Ricans.

With so many different opinions, the whole issue of political status has become more and more complicated over the years. Whatever their eventual choice, Puerto Ricans must address the fact that the country's association with the United States has also led to its economic dependence on the United States.

LUIS MUÑOZ MARÍN

One of Puerto Rico's most important leaders in modern political history was Luis Muñoz Marín, son of Luis Muñoz Rivera.

Born in Puerto Rico, he was educated in the United States and spent some of his youth living in New York. In 1938, he returned to Puerto Rico and formed the Partido Popular Democratico (PPD). He became a very popular figure as he traveled around the countryside drumming up support for the party whose slogan was *Pan, Tierra, y Libertad* (meaning Bread, Land, and Liberty). He was successful in gaining the support of the rural people.

In 1940, he won a seat in the Puerto Rican assembly and from then on became a dominant figure in Puerto Rican politics for the next 24 years. His policy was that the status of Puerto Ricans did not matter—what mattered was their material well-being, and he set about improving this. He also played a major part in Operation Bootstrap, which revitalized the economy and guided it away from dependence on agriculture toward a stronger industrial base.

Muñoz Marín was also successful in persuading Washington to allow Puerto Rico some autonomy. As a result, a provisional Puerto Rican governor replaced the usual U.S. appointee in 1946, and in 1948, Muñoz Marín himself was elected governor.

Muñoz Marín remained governor until 1964 when he retired. However he still remained a strong political figure. In 1966, he played a part in persuading President John F. Kennedy to appoint a commission to look into Puerto Rico's status. Muñoz Marín wanted to retain the commonwealth status rather than join the union. In a plebiscite in 1967, two-thirds of the votes cast supported his call for remaining a commonwealth.

ECONOMY

PUERTO RICO WAS HISTORICALLY an agricultural country producing mainly tobacco, coffee, and sugar—these are often called the "after-dinner commodities." Over the last 40 years, however, it has successfully diversified its economy and now has a flourishing industrial sector based on the production of electronics and pharmaceuticals. This economic turnabout was brought about by Operation Bootstrap.

Puerto Rico today is the most industrialized Caribbean island, with manufacturing and tourism being the two major growth sectors of the economy. Manufacturing now accounts for almost 40% of the economy.

Puerto Rico's income per head is $6,470 per year. Although this is lower than that of Mississippi, the poorest state of the union, it is still higher than the rest of Latin America. Puerto Rico also has one of the highest standards of living in the Caribbean.

Opposite: **Tourist hotels and luxury apartments in San Juan. Tourism is one of Puerto Rico's major sources of revenue. About 80% of tourists come from the United States.**

OPERATION BOOTSTRAP

This began in the mid-1940s to revitalize the economy by building up an industrial sector in Puerto Rico. The government financed and set up many industrial development projects—cement factories, shoe factories, glass manufacturing plants, and fruit processing. By the end of the decade, the plants were profitable and were passed on to private developers.

In the 1950s, the government of Puerto Rico began a massive campaign to attract American investors to the island. By 1955, the drive to lure American firms to the island had been so successful that manufacturing overtook agriculture as the major income generator—500 factories employed 45,000 workers, all eager to improve their standard of living.

In the 1960s, American petrochemical industries began to be attracted to the island. Some labor-intensive industries from the United States also moved to areas in Puerto Rico where wages were lower.

A booming manufacturing sector producing goods for export has resulted in Puerto Rico's becoming an important port and shipment point in the Caribbean.

Great social and economic progress was made in the 1950s and 1960s. Better wages and an improved standard of living quickly established a large middle class in Puerto Rico, whose spending power encouraged more American industries to invest in the country.

In the 1970s, rising oil prices hit Puerto Rico's economy. Economic growth slowed, the construction industry came to a standstill, and many labor-intensive firms left Puerto Rico for countries with lower minimum wages. Then in 1976, another event occurred to reverse this trend and start Puerto Rico on its second phase of rapid expansion.

SECTION 936

In 1976, Section 936 of the United States Internal Revenue Code granted tax exemptions to U.S. companies with investments in Puerto Rico provided they paid 10% of their profits into the national development bank. In return, companies were allowed to keep 25% of their profits tax-free. New taxes were also levied on companies with investments in other Caribbean countries, to ensure that businesses would not shift out of Puerto Rico in search of cheaper labor markets. This made Puerto Rico a tax haven for U.S. businesses.

The industries now attracted to the island were high-technology ones—chemicals, pharmaceuticals, and electronics. By the end of the 1970s, more people were employed in capital-intensive industries than in labor-intensive industries like textiles, clothing manufacture, or rum distilling. By 1989, tax breaks were thought to account for 275,000 jobs, about one-third of Puerto Rico's total employment.

PROS AND CONS OF SECTION 936

Section 936 is debated in the U.S. budget hearings every year. Its advantages for Puerto Rico are obvious.

It provides an enormous pool of money ($15 billion in 1993) to finance investment in industry. It encourages American firms to move to Puerto Rico where they operate free of federal corporate and dividend taxes, as well as enjoy generous tax rates by the Puerto Rican government. Foreign corporations also receive similar tax breaks as well as duty free entry to the U.S. market for goods assembled on the island.

This has also benefited other Caribbean states since Puerto Rico has invested some of its money in neighboring countries by setting up factories there. The disadvantage to the U.S. federal budget is that large amounts of tax revenues are lost.

For Puerto Rico, it also means that its economy is irrevocably tied to the United States. When there is an economic slump in America, it is felt to a greater extent in Puerto Rico. This economic relationship with the United States also has political consequences. If Puerto Rico joins the union, it will lose its tax breaks and become the poorest state of the union. If it becomes independent, the tax breaks will also be lost and Puerto Rico's economy will have to stand on its own.

A rum distillery. Puerto Rico's rum industry grew out of its sugar industry.

PUERTO RICO'S WORKFORCE

Over the last 40 years, Puerto Rico's economy has changed from a highly labor-intensive to a capital-intensive one. As a result, the Puerto Rican workforce has changed from being a rural agricultural population, with only a primary education, to a highly skilled workforce. Over 20% of the population has a college education, and an even higher percentage of the population is bilingual. Every high school graduate is guaranteed a job or job training, and the government has invested millions of dollars in incentives for firms to undertake employee training programs.

Nevertheless, the employment figures are not good. During the 1980s, the unemployment rate was around 20%, though this fell to 15% in the early 1990s.

Puerto Rico has the same minimum wage as the United States, although average wages are still lower than in the United States. About 11% of the population is unionized, mostly those employed in the government sector and in tourism.

PHARMACEUTICALS AND ELECTRONICS

As the United States is an enormous market for pharmaceutical products, many American companies have found it profitable to set up factories in Puerto Rico. The island is now one of the world's leading manufacturers of pharmaceuticals, supplying 7% of the world's demand for pharmaceuticals, and about half the total U.S. market. Puerto Rico's chemical industry now accounts for 36% of its total exports.

Puerto Rico has also developed a strong electronics industry, particularly in producing computer components and printers. About 3,500 people are employed in this sector of the economy.

Both the pharmaceutical and electronics industries find it useful to take advantage of the Caribbean Basin Initiative (CBI), which is funded by Section 936. This allows businesses to set up labor-intensive plants to manufacture semifinished products in other Caribbean countries. The final stages of production take place in Puerto Rico, thus getting the tax benefits of Section 936 and the lower wage bills of other countries.

As Puerto Rico has no oil reserves, a nuclear power plant at Punta Hiquero generates electricity for Puerto Rico's industries and population.

Puerto Rican tobacco is used to make cigars. The main tobacco growing region lies in the hills of eastern Puerto Rico.

AGRICULTURE

In 1940, 31% of the island's net income came from agriculture. But since the industrialization drive known as Operation Bootstrap (described on page 39), agriculture now accounts for a small share of the economy. The agricultural sector has also been plagued by problems of labor shortage and demands for alternative use of the land. The chief agricultural products were and still are sugar, tobacco, and coffee. Other agricultural products include pineapples and coconuts.

Sugarcane production in Puerto Rico reached a peak in the first half of the 20th century, as American businesses brought machinery to make production more profitable. Today, sugar accounts for only 5% of agricultural production. The rum manufacturing industry, which grew out of sugar production, now imports molasses, a sugar by-product from countries with lower minimum wages.

Coffee production was the mainstay of the economy in the 19th century, but declined due to competition from coffee grown in the United States and damage to plants caused by hurricanes. Coffee is still grown in the southeast around Cayey and in the northwest around San Sebastian.

But coffee, tobacco, and sugarcane plantations all have labor problems. Because world cash crop prices keep agricultural wages low, many people prefer to live off welfare payments and food stamps instead of working on farms. As a result, there are not enough agricultural workers to work on these plantations.

With the decline of agriculture, food imports have risen a great deal. To reduce food imports, new ventures in farming have been set up. The island has a team of agronomists who advise farmers on agricultural practices and suggest new ways of making profits. A rice growing program was set up in the 1970s—thousands of acres of land were flattened and a mill was built for the new industry, but the attempt was a failure.

New programs are also being introduced to allow low-paid workers to keep their welfare benefits while they work. Farmers can rent government-owned machinery, warehouses, and packing plants, as well as get low-interest loans to set up their own farms.

Efforts in poultry breeding have been successful. Poultry is the fastest growing farm sector in Puerto Rico, and eventually the island is expected to be self-sufficient in egg production. Other successful projects are in cattle farming, and fruit and vegetable production.

A sugar mill. Sugar is made by boiling sugarcane stems and pressing out the liquid. It is boiled again to form highly concentrated syrup and then spun in huge vats until it forms crystals. Before mechanization, the vats were spun by hand, but in modern refineries, the machines spin at 2,200 revolutions per minute.

PUERTO RICANS

PUERTO RICANS HAVE THEIR ORIGINS in many different parts of the world and this can be seen in the remarkable racial mixture of its people. Their origin can be traced to people of Indian, Spanish, and African background, as well as a number of other sources.

Today, skin color of families that have lived for generations on the island ranges from fair to black, and among Puerto Ricans there are several terms describing different racial types.

The majority of the population has light brown skin and is known as *trigueño* ("trih-GEN-yoh"). A person whose facial features look Indian or Taíno is known as *indio* ("IN-dee-oh"), while a light-skinned person with kinky hair is called *grifo* ("GREE-foh"). People who look mostly Caucasian are known as *blanco* ("BLAHN-coh"). People whose skin color is darkest of all are described as *de color* ("deh cohl-OR"). These are not insulting

Opposite and left: **About 75% of the population are *trigueños*, or people with mixed European and Indian ancestry.**

Puerto Rico has a youthful population. About half of its population is under the age of 22.

terms and no one is offended by them. The word *negro* ("NEHG-roh") means "dear one" and is used regardless of appearance.

Puerto Rico today has a population of 3.6 million, which makes it very densely populated with about 1,000 persons per square mile. Another 2.5 million people of Puerto Rican origin live in the United States. There is also a large shifting population of people who spend time both on the island and in the United States.

A MELTING POT

Evidence of the Taíno heritage can still be seen in the high cheekbones and tawny-colored skin of some inhabitants. The African origin of Puerto Ricans can also still be seen. The Spanish men who first settled the island took wives from the Taíno and African slaves, and a racially mixed majority quickly developed.

Other Europeans also settled here and intermarried. Scottish and Irish farmers came in the 18th and 19th centuries to grow sugarcane. As the Spanish empire began to collapse, the French came from Haiti and from Louisiana after the United States purchased Louisiana from France in 1803.

South Americans fleeing revolution came in the 19th century. When slavery was abolished, immigrant workers arrived from Galicia and the Canary Islands. In the 1840s, a labor shortage brought an influx of Chinese, Italians, Corsicans, and Lebanese. A large community of North Americans also settled in Puerto Rico before the Spanish-American War of 1898.

In more recent times, the Cuban Revolution of 1959 brought many wealthy refugees from middle-class professions or those with their own businesses. The civil war in the Dominican Republic in the 1960s brought a wave of poor refugees.

THE TAÍNO

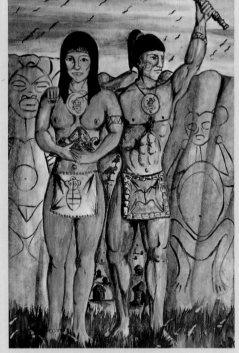

Although the Taíno population was completely wiped out by the Spanish, evidence of their culture and lifestyle still remains.

The Taíno were peaceful farming people living in villages of around 400 people. Their villages or *yucayeques* ("you-kah-YEH-kess") had large houses built from wood and leaves standing around a central square called *batey* ("BAH-teh") where public meetings or religious events took place. Inside the house, *hamaca* ("AH-mah-kah") or hammocks were hung up for sleeping at night. During the day, space was cleared for the weaving, cooking, and other work chiefly done by women.

Taíno men made weapons, hunted, and carved small stone figures. They went mainly naked, while Taíno women wore a cotton skirt called the *nagua* ("NAH-wah").

They worshiped a small pantheon of gods with two major figures representing good and evil. Each village was dominated by a chief or *cacique* ("kah-SIH-keh"). Below him were a group of nobles or privileged men who had several wives and were exempt from the more laborious tasks. Further down in rank were the ordinary men, and at the lowest level of society were the workers or slaves.

The *jíbaro* are the traditional cowboys of Puerto Rican culture. Being peasant farmers, they spent most of the day working in the fields. In the evening, they sang old Spanish songs with their neighbors. To Puerto Ricans, the *jíbaro* is a folk hero, honest and independent, and a reminder of an older, simpler lifestyle.

EL JÍBARO

The *jíbaro* ("HEE-bah-row") are peasant farmers who are descended from runaway Indians, slaves, or deserters from Spanish rule. Living and farming in the mountainous interior of Puerto Rico, they led a simple rural lifestyle.

In the past, the *jíbaro* lived in simple palm-thatched huts called *bohío* ("boh-HEE-oh"), but in modern times they have modern concrete houses with electricity. Like the Taíno Indians, the whole family slept in hammocks hung from the ceiling that were cleared away during the day. They made a living growing subsistence crops such as plantain, bananas, yams, and *yuca* ("YOO-kah," or cassava), and also kept chickens and pigs. Their religion was nominally Catholic, mixed with the religion of the Taíno and the African slaves.

In modern times, there are only a few *jíbaro* living and farming in the country. Many of them have moved to towns to work in factories.

TRADITIONAL *JÍBARO* DRESS

If any form of dress reflects Puerto Rican traditional clothes, it is the simple dress of the *jíbaro*, the peasant farmer.

A broad-brimmed straw hat known as the *pava* ("PAH-vah") keeps the sun out of his eyes as he harvests the sugar. He wears a loose-fitting rough cotton shirt and trousers, and usually goes barefooted. On the farm, the *jíbaro* carries a machete for cutting cane and undergrowth.

Traditional dress for women has a Spanish air to it—a long full dirndl skirt in colorful cotton, with a low-necked peasant blouse and a headscarf, all in bright colors. Lots of chunky jewelry and hoop earrings are also worn.

URBANIZATION

Puerto Rico today is the most urbanized country in the Caribbean. As economic and social progress over the past 40 years have increased employment opportunities and standards of living, a great migration has taken place in the country. People have moved from rural areas to towns in search of jobs and better lives.

About two-thirds of Puerto Ricans live in cities and urban centers today, compared to two-thirds living on farms and in the countryside 50 years ago. Although young Puerto Ricans are mostly well-educated city dwellers nowadays, many come from families who still remember living a rural peasant lifestyle.

Puerto Rico's population of 3.6 million is very unevenly distributed. About half of the population live on the north coast. About one-third live in San Juan and its surrounding satellite towns. The three towns of Bayamón, Guaynabo, and Carolina are within 10 miles of San Juan, and many residents commute to San Juan from these towns. Despite the migration to towns, Puerto Rico still has many tiny villages tucked away in its mountainous interior, some having less than 150 people.

RACE RELATIONS

Intermarriage over the centuries and the blurring of racial differences means that there is very little racial tension on the island. But in the past, some families went to great lengths to protect their racial purity, often insisting that candidates for marriage go through blood purification trials known as *limpieza de sangre* ("lim-pee-EH-zah deh SAHNG-greh") to make sure they had no slave blood. However, education, health, and public places were open to all who could afford it.

In the late 19th century, African Puerto Ricans were leading members of society. José Celso Barbosa was a doctor who served in the cabinet as undersecretary of education in 1897. Rafael Cordero Molina, a shoemaker in the early 19th century, established a school where all poor children who came to him received a free education.

In the town of Loíza, the majority of the population are of African descent. They have not intermarried as much as in other parts of Puerto Rico, so that Loíza today is one of the purest centers of African culture in the country. On the other hand, San Juan has enclaves of exclusively white families living in wealthy areas—they are either immigrants from the United States or descendants of the Spanish colonialists.

From an island of simple agriculturalists Puerto Rico has seen its population swell at an enormous rate. Many of its sons and daughters have made a new life in the United States. Since Puerto Ricans are U.S. citizens, their immigration is not restricted.

PUERTO RICANS IN THE UNITED STATES

In the 1930s, an economic depression led to many Puerto Ricans moving to the United States in search of a better life. This migration lasted until the mid-1960s. When the Korean War ended in 1955, a labor shortage in the United States led thousands of Puerto Ricans to find unskilled but better paid work in the United States. However, when job prospects were bad, migration slowed. In some years during the early 1960s, more Puerto Ricans returned from the United States.

Those who left Puerto Rico for the United States raised their income and had a higher standard of living, but they found that they were disadvantaged by the color of their skin. White skinned Puerto Ricans found that they had an advantage—they found employment and good homes more easily than dark skinned Puerto Ricans.

The early migrants settled in New York City around the Brooklyn Naval Yard and Harlem. By 1930, there were 53,000 Puerto Ricans in New York City. Many also settled in other areas of New York City, often alongside African Americans. Today, there are large Puerto Rican communities in all five boroughs of New York, in New Jersey, New England, Illinois, and California.

Many Puerto Ricans worked as migrant laborers in the East Coast, harvesting sugarcane from January to June, and then returning for the harvest in Puerto Rico. Some were exploited because they could not speak English and worked in extreme conditions. Puerto Ricans still migrate around the United States following the harvests.

LIFESTYLE

THE TRADITIONAL PUERTO RICAN FAMILY is strongly religious, Catholic by faith, and has a great respect for the social hierarchies. Like many third world countries, Puerto Rico had a sudden introduction to the 20th century. It has been transformed from a poor agricultural society to a comparatively wealthy one in a matter of 40 years, well within the memories of many of its citizens.

Puerto Rico shares certain Latin traits with other Latin American countries, particularly the concept of *machismo* ("mah-KHIZ-moh"), or a belief in male superiority. Puerto Ricans also share the Latin idea of fatalism, a belief that life is controlled by some guiding force and that misfortune should be accepted as the will of God. They have a strong sense of dignity and respect, and a fun-loving nature. Puerto Ricans love to be in the company of other people, and being alone too much seems very odd to them.

Opposite: **Most Puerto Ricans today live a fast-paced life, although some small communities still live mainly off the land, in the manner of the traditional *jíbaro*.**

Left: **Re-creation of Taíno village life. The Taínos were farmers and hunters who lived a rural lifestyle.**

THE FAMILY

Of the economic and social changes that have altered Puerto Rican society in the last 40 years, the biggest changes of all have been in the family structure. The traditional family followed a strict Latin pattern. The father was undisputed head of the family, making decisions for the family often without consulting his wife or children. The wife was a silent partner in the marriage, but was respected by her children and honored by her husband as a second mother.

Male children were preferred to female. A husband unable to produce a male heir would be called a *chancletero* ("shahn-cleh-TEH-roh"), an expression meaning a maker of useless things. Boys were brought up to honor *machismo*, while the girls were protected from outside influences for the honor of the family. A girl's virginity was very important to the family honor and would be protected at all costs. Girls might meet their intended husband in chaperoned outings but never alone. Even wives would not go out alone.

At the opposite extreme is the Puerto Rican family unit of the 1990s in New York City, almost half of which are headed by single women, while

NAMES

Like some North American people, Puerto Ricans have three names, but two are surnames. The first name is their given or Christian name, the second is their father's surname, and the third is their mother's maiden name. Confusion often arises when Puerto Ricans and Americans meet, because Americans naturally assume that the last name is the surname. They might say "Hello Senor Acosta" to a man whose name is Jose Lopez Acosta, when in fact his surname is actually Lopez, his father's surname. Puerto Ricans who are not used to such mistakes are sometimes upset at being called by their mother's surname.

When women marry, they can drop their mother's surname before adding their husband's surname to the end of their name. So if Margot Ruiz Marchessi marries a man called Betances, she becomes Margot Ruiz Betances or Margot Ruiz Marchessi de Betances! Many Puerto Ricans in the United States have stopped using their mother's surname to avoid confusion.

others are combinations of members from previous marriages, that is, half-brothers and sisters living with divorced and remarried parents.

The typical modern Puerto Rican family lies in between these two extremes. Women have more freedom of movement, take part in family decisions, earn half the family income, have equal opportunities in education, can divorce if their marriage is not successful, and plan their family size. They have similar expectations as the typical American family, wanting material comfort, a car, a television set, and the best for their children. However, their daughters still experience more restrictions than other American girls.

Marriages on the island are increasing. At one time in Puerto Rico, common-law marriage was fairly common, especially among the poor. Nowadays, social welfare benefits encourage couples to marry, and rising expectations of living among the lower classes make them seek more middle-class lifestyles.

The effect of American values has weakened restrictions on women. Modern women living in the city have their own cars and jobs, and can do almost as much as American women. But in rural areas, there is still pressure on young girls to moderate their behavior in public. Dating is no longer chaperoned and divorce is quite common.

Families tend to do things together, and any occasion can be an excuse for the whole family to get together. Departures and arrivals at the airport are often accompanied by whole families either wishing their relatives goodbye or welcoming them home.

The neighborhood or *barrio* once provided an important social support system for the family and community.

THE EXTENDED FAMILY

The support of extended families has always been important to Latin Americans. To survive the hardships of war or natural disaster, it was customary for several generations to live together. Often, four generations in a family all lived under the same roof.

Although it was once an accepted part of life in Puerto Rican society that the extended family lived at least close by, nowadays this is becoming less common. Most people no longer live in the *barrio* ("BAH-ree-oh") or neighborhood where they grew up, and instead live in areas close to their place of employment. As a result, extended families can no longer call on each other for help as easily as they did before.

Neighbors in the *barrio* were also an important part of traditional society. Since different families may have lived side by side for many generations, they would also have considered themselves part of an extended family.

In the old days, orphaned children would have had their immediate family to turn to, or an uncle out of work would have nieces and nephews to give him food and shelter. The elderly would have ended their days with their children and grandchildren around them.

Today this dependence on the extended family is less likely, and the nuclear family of a father, mother, and two or more children is more common. The old role of the extended family has been taken over by the state, as it has in most other Western countries.

COMPADRES

Although the most important relationships were always within the extended family, an exception to this rule was, and still is, the idea of *compadrazgo* ("cohm-pahd-RAZ-goh"), which means coparenting.

This is similar to the concept of godparents in American society, where close friends or relatives stand at the parents' side at the child's baptism. In Puerto Rico, the *compadre* ("cohm-PAH-dreh," or godfather) and the *comadre* ("coh-MAH-dreh," or godmother) usually are family friends.

The *compadrazgo* relationship goes beyond occasional birthday presents for the child. It is almost a spiritual relationship between the parents, and is close to the native American idea of blood brotherhood or sisterhood. If necessary, a *compadre* may take over the role of the father and bring up the child.

Compadres would not harm one another or be rivals with one another, as the relationship implies deep respect. In older times, a poor family might ask their *patrón* ("pah-TRON") or local landowner to be the child's *compadre*, and the bond between them might be work on the farm in exchange for support and help in hard times.

Organizations aimed at helping new Puerto Rican families in the United States have found the idea of *compadrazgo* useful in helping immigrants settle into American society. An already settled family is encouraged to form a *compadre* relationship with a new immigrant family, and so help them settle into life in America.

Families help each other through a *compadrazgo* relationship, which bonds parents, their child, and its godparent. The godparent plays an active role in bringing up the child and attends important family gatherings.

In common with many other Latin countries, Puerto Rico is still a male-dominated society.

MACHISMO

As in many other Latin cultures, *machismo* is a part of Puerto Rican society. Basically, this is a belief that men are superior to women. A man must display physical strength, bravery, and control over his wife and family. He must maintain the respect and dignity due to him at all times. These things can be lost by a defiant wife or disobedient children, or worse still, by an unfaithful wife.

Ironically, a man's *machismo* can be enhanced by having affairs with other women. Though this behavior is officially disapproved of by other men, it is also secretly admired. A girl, on the other hand, must conduct herself in a proper manner, having perhaps one or two boyfriends approved by her parents, and making the move to a formal courtship quickly before she gets a reputation for loose living.

An important part of *machismo* is the respect of others. This is displayed in formal language and behavior when two men meet and talk. This respect has nothing to do with wealth, since a poor man can have much respect from wealthier neighbors as long as he demonstrates his dignity and pride. A man who spends his time complaining about his problems loses dignity.

Men can be insulted by the terms *nángotado* ("nahng-goh-TAH-doh," meaning stooped), or *aplatado* ("ahp-laht-AH-doh," meaning flattened out). Because of the threat to another man's dignity or *machismo,* Puerto Rican men are careful to avoid open hostility or direct refusals.

POPULATION AND BIRTH CONTROL

In 1898, when Puerto Rico became a United States protectorate, its population stood at barely a million people. But within 40 years, the population had doubled. Family size was very large, especially in rural areas—a rural family might have 10 children or more. This fast population growth worried the administration.

Until 1939, it was a felony to even offer advice on contraception in Puerto Rico. Until the 1960s, it was a sin to do so in this Catholic country. However, the Family Planning Association was set up in 1948. By the late 1960s, it had 60 centers all over the island providing free family planning advice and contraceptives to over 30,000 women.

The big breakthrough in attempts to control population came in 1968 after the election of Governor Luis A. Ferré. Birth control information and subsidized contraceptives were made available throughout the island in government health centers. Today, family size is related to education and income level; middle-class families may have two or three children, while families from poorer, rural backgrounds may have six children.

Different standards of behavior apply to relationships between men and women. While machismo *leads to greater tolerance for promiscuity in men, women are expected to be virtuous and seek serious marriage partners. Protective fathers with* machismo *values may also not allow daughters to date for too long before settling down.*

An increase in the number of women working has altered the traditional structure of Puerto Rico's society and way of life, especially in the cities.

OTHER VALUES

Fatalism has always been an important aspect of traditional Puerto Rican culture. This is the belief that since life is controlled by supernatural forces, people should accept their fate. Good fortune should be accepted gladly, but if misfortune occurs, that too should be accepted without complaint.

For the rich people in Puerto Rican society, this can justify wealth, while the poor comfort themselves by saying that misfortunes are the will of God. However, like other Latin values, this is being eroded by modern institutions, such as trade unions, and the breakup of the old landowner-worker relationship.

Another strong belief among Latin men is that of *personalismo* ("per-son-ahl-IZ-moh")— the individual worth of each man. This works against group activities such as trade unionism. Individuals will often put their trust in one powerful man rather than a group of peers. People in Puerto Rico tend to support and vote for individuals rather than sets of ideas belonging to one political party or another. This characteristic also leads to a strong preference for personal contact, especially in business.

Puerto Ricans also believe in bending rules to suit the circumstances. A common expression, *ay bendito* ("aye ben-DEE-toh"), which literally means "blessed be the Lord," is also used to mean something like "have a heart." It is very often used with traffic policemen by people caught speeding who want to avoid being fined.

These Puerto Rican values and characteristics are often quite difficult for Americans to appreciate. The concept of *personalismo* and a strong belief in bending rules make many Western business practices, with their rules and regulations, quite foreign to Puerto Ricans.

LIFE IN THE COUNTRYSIDE

Two generations ago, two-thirds of Puerto Ricans lived in the countryside, visiting the nearest *pueblo* ("poo-EHB-loh") or small town for shopping trips. The traditional rural inhabitant was the *jíbaro*. Nowadays, only one-third of the people live in rural areas. Even so, there are many small farming villages and communities in the interior of the country that are far removed from city life.

Life in the countryside is slow, with the traditional protective attitudes to women and young girls. The work is physically hard, and as agricultural work is poorly paid, there is no middle class.

Traditionally, the Puerto Rican rural community existed on subsistence crops, supplemented by work on the local landowners' fields. After 1898, when American corporations bought up the sugar plantations and turned them into large-scale businesses, the structure of rural life changed. The independent *jíbaro* could no longer negotiate with his local *patrón,* since the new landowners were corporations in the United States.

Rural society changed quickly into large groups of laborers negotiating as a group with foremen, especially in the coastal plains that were more profitable to farm. But in the mountainous areas where coffee plantations are cultivated, the traditional lifestyle remains.

Puerto Ricans have one of the highest ratios of cars to adults in the world, which makes driving in the city hazardous. There are many public buses and a system of nontraditional transportation, in which fares can be negotiated.

63

CITY LIFE

A large middle class can be found in cities and towns, living comfortable lives with good employment prospects. The capital, San Juan, is surrounded by a number of satellite towns from which residents can easily commute to work. Like American cities, it has shopping malls, convenience stores, leisure centers, parks, and other amenities. Houses in San Juan are designed and built for nuclear families, with carports and yards. Land has become the largest factor in the cost of a home, and housing developments now include many apartment complexes and low-cost housing projects designed to house the poor. There are also exclusive and expensive complexes with carefully protected doors and windows.

Many people living in towns have kept up their ties to their rural roots, and a regular weekend or vacation activity is to travel into the countryside to visit relatives. Most families own a car, and there is an efficient public transportation system that travels across the mountains and into the small villages.

SLUMS

In the past 30 years, the massive migration to cities and towns has resulted in the development of *arrabales* ("ah-rah-BAH-yes," meaning slums or shantytowns).

One such slum area is La Perla, a shantytown in San Juan. It is built on a public beach and is separated from the city by the old city walls. Water and electricity are supplied by the government, which also provides building materials and garbage collection services.

With housing shortages and costs so high, there is little point in evicting people who at least have a community to live in. La Perla's residents are mostly unemployed and living on welfare payments, but many have refrigerators, television sets, and cars. This brightly colored settlement is now one of San Juan's tourist attractions.

HEALTH CARE

When the first Puerto Rican men were called up to serve in the United States Army in World War II, over 78% of them failed the medical test. At that time, the general health of Puerto Ricans was very low, as most of them could not afford health care. In 1940, there was only one doctor for every 4,000 citizens.

Since then, great improvements in health care have been made—the number of doctors has increased, and hospitals and clinics have been set up in towns and rural areas. Much of Puerto Rico's health care is covered by medical insurance, while the poor still receive help in paying their medical bills. Another reason for the better health record is that diet has also improved enormously.

Improved health care has increased Puerto Rican life expectancy from 47 years in 1940 to 70 years in modern times.

A slum house on Guaja-taca beach. Shanties are built from corrugated iron and wood, often with no sanitation. Unfortu-nately, some of these slums have also become centers of drugs and crime.

The Puerto Rican government has invested heavily in raising educational levels in Puerto Rico. As a result, Puerto Rico has among the most educated people in the Caribbean. Its literacy rate has risen to 90%, compared to just 69% in 1940.

EDUCATION

In the early years of American rule, the American governors of Puerto Rico believed that the English language and American culture were the keys to the island's future. English was made the language of instruction in schools, despite the fact that neither the teachers nor the pupils could understand or speak it.

This situation remained until 1948, when the United States turned over the administration of the education system to a locally-appointed commissioner of education. Spanish was then officially returned as the language of instruction in Puerto Rico and English became compulsory as a second language. In modern Puerto Rico, speaking English is essential

THE YOUNG LORDS

In the mid-1960s, when students virtually all over the world discovered the effectiveness of student protest, Puerto Rican students in Puerto Rico and in major cities in the United States discovered that they could make a point by demonstrations.

One such group active in New York City were the Young Lords, who became concerned with the lack of educational opportunities for young Puerto Ricans. On one occasion, they occupied a New York City church and used it to set up an early morning educational program for children. For a while, another group of Young Lords caused the City University of New York to close for a period in 1969.

Their efforts brought the plight of Puerto Rican students to public attention, made Puerto Rican voters aware that they could influence the educational system, and helped bring about bilingual programs in the city. They were also responsible for the establishment of several Puerto Rican study programs in the universities around New York City.

in most jobs. In cities and towns, most people are bilingual in Spanish and English.

Education on the island has gone through an enormous change, from being available to just a small privileged portion of society in 1898 to almost universal primary education. A large proportion of the population graduates from high school. Changing educational standards have resulted in an increasing number of college graduates in Puerto Rico's workforce.

There are many flourishing and successful private schools on the island that have a high success rate in getting students into the government-run university. Ironically, poorer students who are educated in the public school system get poorer grades and lose out on places in the University of Puerto Rico. They then must seek places at the less prestigious but more expensive private colleges.

In modern Puerto Rico, a new educational problem is in teaching Spanish to the children of returned emigrants.

Education is the key to a better life in Puerto Rico. About 80% of Puerto Ricans who are employed have more than 13 years of education, while 70% of those who are unemployed have less than 12 years of education.

LIFE IN THE UNITED STATES

Almost 40% of all people of Puerto Rican descent live in the United States. For some Puerto Ricans, life in the United States is just a temporary measure to make enough money or provide the children with a good education. When these are satisfied, they return to Puerto Rico to live. Second generation Puerto Ricans who were born in New York City but have returned to the island are called "Nuyoricans."

Many people disillusioned with American life have also returned and discovered that their children are homesick for Chicago or New York. Many of them have problems adapting to the language and culture when they return. Puerto Ricans who have settled permanently in the United States find that the second generation faces the challenge of adjusting between American culture and the culture of their parents at home.

Puerto Ricans make up one-fourth of all students in New York City's public schools. New York City has the greatest concentration of Puerto Ricans in the United States.

Women often experience the most difficulties in adjusting to American life. Men, on the other hand, become involved in the new society through their workplace, while children adapt quickly in the school system. Housewives, on the other hand, often remain in a largely Spanish-speaking neighborhood, and those who do not work may find great difficulty in adjusting to the new language and society.

Many schools in New York City have introduced bilingual teaching programs to make sure that Puerto

Rican students are not disadvantaged. Although many students are now third generation New Yorkers, the percentage of Puerto Ricans who graduate is still below the national average. California has the highest level of Puerto Ricans in professional and managerial positions, and the highest incomes among Puerto Ricans in America.

WELFARE PAYMENTS

With up to 15% of the population of Puerto Rico unemployed, welfare payments have for a long time formed a large part of public expenditure in Puerto Rico and Washington,

In rural areas, many people prefer to stay on welfare instead of taking low-paid agricultural work.

D.C. However, the U.S. government contributes a smaller amount of money toward welfare payments in Puerto Rico than it does to poor states such as Mississippi. The U.S. contribution is in the form of food stamps and Medicaid, and is supplemented by the Puerto Rican government.

These welfare payments to the unemployed and disabled, although low by American standards, keep the unemployment rate high—as soon as someone finds work, even low-paid work, they lose their rights to welfare payments.

If Puerto Rico joined the union, welfare payments would be brought up to U.S. standards and the unemployed would receive a great boost to their income with higher welfare checks. On the other hand, the loss of companies who operate in Puerto Rico because of the tax concession would mean that unemployment would almost certainly rise even higher, making even more people dependent on welfare.

RELIGION

ALTHOUGH PUERTO RICO IS mainly a Catholic country, its religious beliefs have been influenced by the Taíno religion and the spiritualism brought by African slaves. This makes Puerto Rican Catholicism different from that of other Catholic countries. Worship of individual saints is also much stronger and more common than in other Catholic communities.

CATHOLICISM

The Catholic faith came to Puerto Rico with Spanish settlers, who were later followed by priests spreading the Christian religion and converting the natives.

In the 17th century, the Catholic faith spread quickly throughout the island. Thatched roof churches were built in every settlement. The church quickly became just as prominent a building in the town square as the municipal hall. Today, about 99% of the population of Puerto Rico is Christian, with about 80% Roman Catholic.

TAÍNO RELIGION

The Taíno Indians believed in a supreme creator or god whom they called Yocahu, and who lived high in the central chain of mountains on the mountain now called El Yunque. They believed in a spirit world where all natural things had a soul, and spirits lived in rivers, trees, and stones. Their equivalent of the devil was called *Jurakan* ("hoo-rah-KAHN") and he

Opposite: **The Cathedral of Our Lady of Guadalupe in Ponce, Puerto Rico's second largest city.**

Above: **Four centuries of Spanish rule have led to a predominantly Catholic population in Puerto Rico.**

71

AFRICAN INFLUENCE

When African slaves were brought to the island from the east coast of Africa, they brought with them some elements of their religion, including a kind of animism. This can still be seen in religious festivals at Loíza, where masqueraders wear masks and costumes similar to those worn by the Yoruba tribe in Nigeria.

could call forth terrible powers of nature to harm the people. It is from this Taíno word that the modern English word hurricane is derived. Lesser gods called *cemi* ("SAY-mee") were also worshiped.

Each family and village had their own carved wooden god or stone image of their *cemi*. The Taíno believed in the afterlife and buried their dead carefully, burying their requirements, such as food, water, weapons, and jewelry, with them. Although none of the original Taíno survive, some of their spiritual beliefs are still seen in the *jíbaro*.

THE CHURCH AND LIFE'S BIG EVENTS

The majority of the island's population practice a very personal form of Catholicism. Unlike other Latin Catholic countries, daily worship, mass, and confession are not a big part of Puerto Ricans' faith. Instead most homes have pictures or carved statues of particular saints whom people call on when they need help and protection. An individual may turn to the Virgin Mary for comfort in times of trouble and keep a statue for protection.

Most children are baptized by a priest. Parents often seek people to form a *compadre*, or godparent, relationship for their child. As the child grows up, it is surrounded by statues representing the holy family and saints. Children are taught to fear *el diablo* ("el dee-AH-bloh") or the devil.

In daily life, people use religious expressions very often, such as *Si Dios quiere*, ("see DEE-oh kee-AIR-eh," meaning "God willing") or *ay bendito*

A fisherman seeks blessings from the saints to ensure a good catch.

("aye ben-DEE-toh," meaning "blessed be the Lord"). At age seven, Catholic children make their first Holy Communion. At puberty, they are confirmed in the church when they take another name, usually after a saint for whom they have developed a special reverence.

Traditional church weddings with white dresses are common among wealthier families, but among the poor, common-law marriages not formalized by the church also take place. The children born to these families can still be baptized in church.

Puerto Ricans also seek blessings when they start a new business. Whenever a new shop or office opens, priests are called upon to perform a blessing at the opening ceremony.

RELIGION

OTHER FORMS OF CHRISTIANITY

Among the other religions represented in Puerto Rico is Judaism. San Juan has a small Jewish community of a few hundred families.

The Catholic Church's emphasis on suffering life's adversities and being rewarded for goodness in heaven rather than on earth explains why many people in Latin American countries, including Puerto Rico, have suffered poverty without much complaint. Protestant values, on the other hand, indicate that reward can come while still on earth and that hard work should be followed by material happiness.

For a long time, Protestantism was considered heretical by the Catholic Church and was not allowed in any of its colonies until the 19th century. The first Protestant churches were established in Ponce and on Vieques Island after Queen Victoria of Britain asked for special dispensation for English families who had settled there. Later, an Episcopalian church was set up by Americans settling in Puerto Rico.

DEATH CUSTOMS

Death is marked both by a religious service and by personal custom.

In rural areas, dying people receive the church's last rites and are also visited by all their friends and neighbors, who keep a night-long *velada* ("veh-LAH-dah") or vigil as the dying pass their last hours. The *velada* is held in the home of the dying person, with the women inside the house and the men outside. After a death, another night-long *velada* is held, also with the men outside and the women inside. Food and cane rum might be served, but the event never becomes loud. In some regions, the rosary is said for nine nights following the funeral service, which is conducted by a priest.

In the cities, as with other events, the observation of a death is more like a funeral in North America. A religious service is followed by a brief family gathering at the deceased's home.

74

After the American takeover in 1898, Protestant communities in the United States saw Puerto Rico as a ground for conversions. Today there are less than half a million Protestants in Puerto Rico, the majority of whom belong to one of the revivalist movements. Among the Protestant sects in Puerto Rico are many evangelist groups, including Jehovah's Witnesses, Mormons, Methodists, Episcopalians, and Baptists.

The Pentecostal church has found support on the island. The church practices faith healing and baptism, and members seek to be one with the Holy Spirit. Meetings of these groups are small and often held in homes or local stores. Members of the congregation are encouraged to describe their faith and experiences. An interesting event that sometimes occurs during meetings is called "talking in tongues," when congregation members feel they have been taken over by the Holy Spirit. Services also include lively singing, and members are encouraged to abstain from drinking and smoking and to obey certain dress codes. Pastors of Pentecostal churches are often local people instead of ministers sent from the United States.

A local form of evangelism built up during the 1940s around a woman named Mita, who saw the improvement of conditions for her congregation as part of her mission on earth. The Mita sect runs businesses and provides work opportunities for its members. Mita sect churches were opened in New York City and Chicago. Mita died in 1970, but her church lives on.

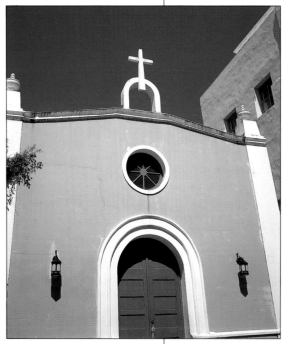

The Roman Catholic San Juan Church.

SPIRITUALISM

Among simpler people of the island, a belief in the "evil eye" can still be found. Infant children, especially pretty ones, wear an amulet of black beads to protect them from harm.

Spiritualism exists alongside the more established religions. It is practiced by both Catholics and Protestants along with the more common aspects of Christian religion.

Every town or city has at least one spiritual medium who may be a housewife, a truck driver, or a member of a profession, but who is believed to have special powers. These special powers include contacting the spirits of the dead to ask for protection and guidance, and predicting the future. Spiritualists even call on pillars of the Catholic Church such as the saints for their guidance. Their homes are often filled with pictures and statues of saints and other religious figures. Customers of spiritualists come from all levels of society, from rich to poor.

Other spiritualists use natural medicine to help the sick. In every town, shops called *botánica* ("boh-TAHN-ih-kah") sell herbal medicines used by spiritualists. Some of the herbs are harmless, others can be dangerous, but several have been discovered by modern medicine to be cures for the ailments for which the spiritualists prescribe them. Medicines can be made into herbal teas called *tisanas* ("tih-SAHN-ahs") or mixed with alcohol as a rub.

These shops also sell candles, incense, and other things associated with the Catholic church, as well as charms, amulets, and magic powders. They are equally popular in cities like New York and other American cities with Puerto Rican neighborhoods, where they attract both a wide variety of people from all classes of life, and even born-and-bred New Yorkers.

Some old spiritual beliefs and ceremonies include the *rosario* ("roh-ZAHR-ee-oh"), where a shrine is set up for a sick person and the family and neighbors pray to the saints to help the person recover. Another traditional spiritualist ceremony is the *rogativa* ("roh-gah-TEE-vah"), where a whole neighborhood turns out in the street to pray for something. If there is a drought, for example, everyone joins together to pray for rain.

In remote areas of the island, particularly around Loíza, there are more obvious signs of the animistic religions of the African ancestors. People carry with them a *resurgado* ("reh-zer-GAHR-oh") or talisman that keeps the evil eye or witchcraft away. In the old days, simple people believed in love potions or spells, but the influence of modern medicines and satellite television has caused the disappearance of many of those old beliefs.

A wall mural shows a masked figure from African tradition in a Christian ceremony.

PUERTO RICO

JOANNES EST NOMEN EJVS

LANGUAGE

UNTIL AMERICAN RULE, LANGUAGE in Puerto Rico was a simple affair. Everyone spoke a form of Spanish that was understood by Spanish-speaking people, but which still had certain differences from original Spanish. No English was spoken then. When the first American soldiers tried to communicate with the people, the main means of communication was nods, smiles, and basic sign language.

In modern Puerto Rico, English has become the passport to job success. It is learned in many different ways, from television, on the streets, and in the schools. An interesting result of mixing Spanish and English is Spanglish, a lively dialect formulated on the streets of New York City and brought back by returning Puerto Ricans. It is a mixture of Spanish grammar, English vocabulary, and some New York City street talk.

SPANGLISH

Spanglish is an odd mixture of English and Spanish that evolved in Puerto Rico and among Latin communities in the United States.

It is made up of words borrowed from English, most of them being either slang words or technological words describing some new idea or object. Some words borrowed from English date from before 1898, such as *ron* ("rohn"), the Spanish word for rum that came from the British Antilles in the 1870s. Another English word, foxtrot, which was the name of a dance popular in the 1920s, has entered Puerto Rican Spanish and now means "fight."

Many English words, such as bar, record, standard, and ticket, have moved intact into Spanglish. An even more interesting effect of bilingualism and Spanglish is the way Puerto Ricans use two languages in one sentence, such as "*se está brushing his teeth,*" or "*tu miras funny.*"

Opposite: **A souvenir poster of Puerto Rico.**

SPANISH

The 16th century wave of Spanish colonization in the Caribbean and South America meant that Spanish was the dominant language of this region. Even today, the language spoken by people in Central America, some West Indian islands, and the Caribbean coast of South America is still a form of Spanish. Although the accents and pronunciation in these former Spanish colonies are different from those of modern Spain, the language is still recognizable as Spanish.

Puerto Rican Spanish has its own unique characteristics. One of the features of its language is that many consonants that should be pronounced in Spanish by using the front of the mouth, are actually softened and pronounced in the back of the mouth. For example, the rolled Spanish "r,"

Unlike other Caribbean countries like Jamaica, where pidgin dialects have emerged, Puerto Rican Spanish is still very much like Spanish spoken elsewhere in the world. It can still be understood by a Spanish-speaking person from outside the country.

formed by flicking the tongue against the back of the teeth, has become softer sounding, like a French word. Another example is that the letter "s" is not pronounced. This makes it difficult for a foreigner to tell if the person is speaking in the singular or plural. In Puerto Rico, the word *gracias* sounds more like *grahiah* ("GRAH-hee-ah"), and *las madres*, meaning the mothers, sounds like *la madre* ("lah MAH-dreh," or the mother). Similarly, Spanish words with a double "l" are pronounced like an English-sounding "y," so that the word *tortilla* is pronounced "tor-TEE-yah." Another interesting feature is that words ending in "ado" are sometimes pronounced without the "d" sound. It is a question of class, the dropped "d" being common and the inserted "d" being the standard pronunciation.

Some words whose origin is uniquely Puerto Rican are *pon* ("pohn," meaning hitchhike), *chevere* ("shey-VAIR-eh," meaning well done) and *agallarse* ("ahg-ahl-YAR-seh," meaning to become angry).

USTED AND TU

Different languages have different ways of expressing politeness and respect. In English, respect for someone might appear in the way you address the person, for example by using "sir" or "ma'am," or expressions of politeness such as "please" or "would you" rather than a simple command.

One way of expressing politeness that does not exist in English but is very important in Spanish is in the word "you." In Spanish, *usted* ("oo-STED") is used in the plural and *tu* ("too") in the singular. But if Puerto Ricans wish to show respect, they will say *usted*. When close friends speak informally, they could use *tu*. In a *compadrazgo* relationship, in order to show the formal nature of the relationship and the respect between the parties, the word *usted* is used.

TAÍNO INFLUENCES

According to legend, when the Carib attacked the Taíno, they carried off some Taíno women. These Taíno women, although now living with the Carib, still spoke the Taíno language and taught it to their daughters, whom they kept with them in the home. Their sons, however, went out to work with their Carib fathers and learned the language of the Carib. As a result, the Carib had two languages—one spoken by the women of the tribe and another spoken by the men.

Although the Taíno have not survived in Puerto Rico, something remains of their influence. Many names of Puerto Rican towns, such as Mayagüez, Manatí, and Arecibo, are of Taíno origin. The town of Caguas is named after a Taíno chief, Caguax, who once ruled over the valley where the town is now located.

A bus stop street sign in San Juan.

Some words have come from the Taíno language, traveled through Spanish, and entered the English language. The English word hurricane comes from the Taíno name for the devil, *Jurakan.* The word hammock comes from the Taíno style of bed, the *hamaca.* Other words of Taíno origin are tobacco, canoe, maracas, maize, and savannah. The word key, meaning small island, such as in Florida Keys, also comes from the Taíno language.

It is believed that about 500 words in Puerto Rican Spanish are of Taíno origin, many of them being words to do with plants and animals. The word *guajana* ("goo-ah-CHAR-nah") describes the tips of the sugarcane stalk. It is a Taíno word found only in Puerto Rico, unlike many other Taíno words found in the Dominican Republic, Cuba, and other former Spanish colonies in the Caribbean.

AFRICAN WORDS

The language of the west African slaves that the Spanish brought to Puerto Rico has also had a lasting effect on the island's language.

Although the African slaves lasted much longer under Spanish rule than the Taíno, the African influence on language was less than the Taíno influence. One theory to explain this is that the slaves brought to the Spanish empire had been taken from different tribes in various areas of Africa and might not have spoken the same language. The only language they had in common was probably the Spanish they learned from their masters.

Among the African words that survive in Puerto Rico's language today are *bemebe* ("bay-MEH-bay," meaning big lip), *quimbombo* ("keem-BOM-boh," or okra), and *guneo* ("goo-NEY-oh," or banana). The name of a ceremony that takes place after the death of an infant, *baquine* ("bah-KEEN-eh"), is also of African origin, as is the ritual itself.

Above: **Roadside signs in English and Spanish cater to a bilingual population.**

Opposite: **A young boy delivers newspapers.**

THE ADVENT OF ENGLISH

When the Americans arrived in 1898, virtually no one in Puerto Rico spoke any English. The United States administration in Puerto Rico set about changing this by introducing English in schools.

Under the Clark Policy (named after the first education commissioner, Victor Clark), English was made the language of instruction in schools, even though the teachers and pupils spoke no English and had no English textbooks.

Since then various methods have introduced bilingualism to the country. For a time, Spanish was the language of instruction in the lower grades in school, with both languages being used in the middle grades, and English in the higher grades. At present, Spanish is the language of instruction in schools, and English is taught as a foreign language in daily lessons.

English has now become the language through which successful students go on to university or succeed in commerce and business. Many English language courses and night classes are offered by private schools that attract customers by pointing out the economic advantage of English.

Nowadays, more and more Puerto Ricans are bilingual in English and Spanish. But the return of many Puerto Rican families from the United States has raised a new language problem—their children are often more proficient in English than Spanish, and this has led to new evening classes being arranged, this time in Spanish.

THE PRESS

Several English and Spanish newspapers are published in Puerto Rico. *El Mundo* and *El Nuevo Día* are Spanish publications with a conservative point of view. *El Nuevo Día* is the most pro-statehood of the two and is more popular. They are both tabloids with lots of gossip and book excerpts. A third and newer newspaper, *El Reportero*, has a smaller readership.

The most radical newspaper currently in publication is the *Claridad*, which began as the mouthpiece of the pro-independence movement. It has gained readership over the years due to several important stories about government and private industry scandals. It is read largely by the young and by supporters of Communism.

An English paper is the *San Juan Star*. Its readership is mainly the English-speaking and expatriate community. It is mildly pro-statehood and much of its coverage is North American. American newspapers such as *The New York Times*, *The Washington Post*, and a Spanish publication, *El Diario*, are also available.

ARTS

PUERTO RICO'S STRONG artistic tradition has been shaped by its Taíno, Spanish, and African heritage. Cultural traditions are preserved in its daily life, the media, museums, and the lively contributions of writers and musicians. Puerto Rican arts and culture have also influenced American arts through the island's emigrants and its close economic and political association with the United States.

FOLK ART

Folk art in Puerto Rico ranges from making masks for festivals to gaily decorated hammocks, tatted cloth, and saint carvings.

Veigante ("veh-GAHN-teh") masks are made from coconuts or wood for the period of Lent. They were originally made in the shape of devils to scare the local people into repenting during Lent. Although these masks are still carved, most of them are now more for tourists than Puerto Ricans, and animal heads are more frequently seen than devils.

Another Puerto Rican craft is the art of tatting, where threads of twine are drawn into patterns and knotted together to give a lace-like effect. The traditional hammock of the Taíno Indians has been given this modern treatment. In the shops of San Juan, beautiful, gaily patterned hammocks are decorated with tatted borders looking like delicate lacework. These borders are called *mundillos* ("moon-DEE-johs"). Tatting is widely practiced around Aguadilla on the northwest coast. The traditional *pava* hat worn by *jíbaros* is also made there.

Opposite: **A *pava* hat-maker.**

Above: **Carved *veigante* masks.**

A modern painting reproduces Taíno art and sculpture. Remains of Taíno art have been found in stone carvings dating back over 500 years.

Another traditional craft learned from the Spanish is the art of leather working, which mainly serves the tourist industry. Cattle rearing was once a major industry in Puerto Rico and leather items are still made by local craftsmen. They can be found along with imported leather items in the craft shops of San Juan.

Making musical instruments is another craft form that flourishes in Puerto Rico. Local craftsmen make instruments such as the *tres* ("trehs"), *cuatro* ("coo-AH-troh"), and *seis* ("sehs"), which are guitars with three, four, and six strings. Taíno percussion instruments such as the *quiros* ("KEE-rohs," or rattle), the *claves* ("CLAH-vehz"), and the *güiro* ("GWEE-roh") are still made in the traditional way.

Early in Puerto Rico's history, the Taíno made beautiful carved wooden thrones called *duhos* ("doo-hohs") for their chiefs, as well as carved wooden boxes and bowls. The Taíno were also the original people who made hammocks out of woven and dyed cloth.

Saint carving is a very important Puerto Rican craft. Each family owns a number of *santos* ("SAHN-tohs", or carved wooden saints) that are often handed down in the family from generation to generation. Just about every saint in Christianity is represented somewhere

on the island. Early statues are delicately carved in the Spanish style, but later ones have moved away from Spanish influence toward a more primitive style. These wooden carvings are often decorated with small silver medallions in the shape of parts of the body. The medallions are placed there by formerly sick people who attribute their recovery to the healing powers of the saint.

The art of carving wooden saints was traditionally passed down from generation to generation. Today, few young people learn this art, raising fears that it may slowly die out.

A dance troupe wearing Taíno ceremonial dress.

MUSIC AND DANCE

Puerto Rican Latin music is world famous. It evolved from Spanish dances and songs and was influenced by the rhythm of African music brought by slaves.

Much of the essential sounds of Puerto Rican music can be traced to Taíno and African origins. Taíno music used mainly percussion instruments: hollowed-out tree trunks were beaten with sticks and accompanied by shaking gourds with beans or stones inside. The Taíno called these *maracas* ("mah-RAHK-ehs"), and their distinctive sound can still be heard in modern Puerto Rican music. Another Taíno instrument, the *güiro*, is a carved and notched gourd played by drawing a stick across it.

The Spanish danced to songs in the *danza* ("DAHN-zah") style, similar to ballroom dancing. This was most popular in the 19th century and was performed by an orchestra with string and wind instruments. Puerto Rico's national anthem, *La Borinqueña*, is a *danza* that has been adapted to solemn music.

The peasant version of this Spanish-style music, called the *danzón* ("dahn-ZON"), is more uptempo. This music also evolved in the early 20th century under the influence of other Latin countries into dance tunes such as the mazurka, merengue, and mambo.

In modern times Puerto Rico's major musical contribution has been in *salsa* ("SAHL-zah") music. The person who probably did most to create this sound is Tito Puente, born in Spanish Harlem in New York City to Puerto Rican parents. Characteristic of his work and of all *salsa* music is the use of the *timbales* ("tim-BAH-les"), or open-ended drums played with untapered sticks. *Salsa* is typically full of African rhythm. Puente has recorded many albums and is popular throughout the United States and the Caribbean.

Younger *salsa* composers and performers include Willie Colón, Hector Lavoe, the Fania All Stars, and Willie Rosarion. A young pop version of the music is performed by Menudo, who became famous in the 1980s and are still very popular in the United States and Central and South America.

In classical music, Puerto Rico has benefited greatly from Pablo Casals, the world-famous cellist. He was born in Spain to a Puerto Rican mother and settled in Puerto Rico in 1957 at the age of 81. He instituted a world music festival in Puerto Rico that continued after his death in 1973. He also founded a music conservatory and a symphony orchestra that is among the best in the Caribbean.

There are several types of traditional songs played at certain events or festivals in Puerto Rico. The *bomba y plena* ("bom-bah yih PLAY-nyah") is improvised music played on percussion instruments in cafés and public squares. Another traditional song is the *décima* ("DEH-see-mah"). It can be played on three-, four-, or six-stringed guitars. The song has two parts—one singer sings the first verse, followed by a second singer improvising the next verse. The *décima* also has African roots that have been traced to the Yoruba people in Nigeria.

Justino Díaz is one of the leading bass singers in the New York Metropolitan Opera. He is Puerto Rico's finest male vocalist who has sung all over the world.

Bomba dancers dance to African-influenced music and rhythm.

Although much of Puerto Rico's fine art is best appreciated in San Juan, the rural community is not neglected. Under a government project called Operación Serenidad, *a traveling library and a mobile museum go from town to town, and a theater on wheels brings drama to remote villages. The Institute of Puerto Rican Culture also sponsors concerts, lectures, ballets, art exhibitions, plays, and films all over the island.*

FINE ARTS

The first Puerto Rican painter to gain recognition was José Campeche, who lived from 1752 to 1809 in the tiny fortress town of San Juan, painting religious paintings and commissions from local dignitaries. He painted thousands of oil paintings, but few of them survive. Two of his religious paintings are in the museum at Ponce, while his portrait of Governor Ustariz hangs in the Institute of Puerto Rican Culture in San Juan.

Francisco Oller y Cesterro, who lived from 1833 to 1917, left Puerto Rico for France and became a part of the Impressionist movement. He became close friends with Paul Cézanne, the French impressionist artist, and spent his spare time singing as a church sexton to finance his painting. One of his paintings hangs in the Louvre museum in Paris and many others can be seen in Puerto Rico's museums. One of his works, considered by some to be his best, is called *El Velorio*, a mourning for the death of a young child.

JOSÉ FELICIANO

In pop music, José Feliciano is the most famous Puerto Rican on the world music stage. Born in Puerto Rico, he suffered from glaucoma, which made him blind from birth. When he was five years old, his family moved to New York City, where he learned to play the guitar, other string instruments, keyboards, the harmonica, and the trumpet. He began working as a singer and musician in the coffee shops of Greenwich Village in his teens, and by 1965, he made his first album, which was a moderate success among Spanish Americans. In 1968, he rose to world fame with the song, "Light My Fire." He performed live at the opening of the fifth game of the 1968 baseball World Series in front of 53,000 spectators in Detroit and millions more worldwide, singing his famous version of *The Star-Spangled Banner.*

Oller paved the way for other artists to use Puerto Rican themes for their paintings. Miguel Pou and Ramon Frade both painted scenes from Puerto Rican life in the early years of this century.

After World War II, artists such as Lorenzo Homar, J.A. Torres Martinó, and Rafael Tufino founded the Center for Puerto Rican Art in San Juan. Puerto Rican art began to attract foreign collectors and buyers, and more art galleries were opened.

Another art form, silkscreen printing, was used to produce the first cinema posters and limited editions of artists' works as their reputation grew. The new generation of artists, some of whom were born in New York and had returned to the island, also experimented with woodcut and linocut techniques. In linocut, the picture to be printed is carved into linoleum mounted on a block of wood. This is dipped in paint and stamped on the paper.

In the days of pop art, Antonio Martorell grew in prominence, producing playing cards with political cartoons and designing an underground shopping center, called the Ondergraun, for teenagers.

In the last 30 years, many Puerto Rican artists have studied abroad and brought the influence of other parts of the world to their style of painting. Some of these include Myrna Baez, Ivette Cabrera, and Consuelo Gotay.

A poster advertising an exhibition on the artistic heritage of the Taino in Puerto Rico.

LITERATURE

In the early years of Puerto Rico's history, folk tales and nature poetry made up the body of literature on the island. But in modern times, social changes have brought more contemporary literature. Modern writers write about the problem of nationality, the loss of innocence as the *jíbaro* becomes a rarity, urban poverty, and loss of the old values that held society together.

Early writings that emerged from Puerto Rico are letters and histories written by the early Spanish settlers or by native men who left the island and wrote about their travels. In 1849, a sociological story about the islanders was written by Manuel A. Alonso, a medical student from Puerto Rico who lived in Spain. He used prose and poetry and wrote about the daily life of the islanders.

It was not until the 1890s that islanders began to produce Puerto Rican novels. Manuel Zeno Gandia was the first novelist from the island. His most important novel was called *La Charca*, which means stagnant pool and symbolizes the author's view of an island society held back from progress by the church and by feudal landlords.

In the 20th century, Enrique Laguerre began writing novels on Puerto Rican society. René Marqués is the island's most famous writer and has written novels, short stories, and plays. His best known work is *The Ox Cart*, a play about a simple farming family moving to New York and struggling to adjust to their new lives.

Laguerre and other modern writers such as Pedro Juan Soto and José Luis Gonzáles wrote about Puerto Ricans' experiences of living in the United States. Soto's first book, *Spiks,* contains a collection of short stories written in Spanish and Spanglish about Puerto Rican families and society in New York City.

Piri Thomas is a writer of Puerto Rican descent in the United States. He discovered his writing talent while serving a prison sentence for attempted armed robbery. His autobiography, Down These Mean Streets*, is about his life in Spanish Harlem in New York City.*

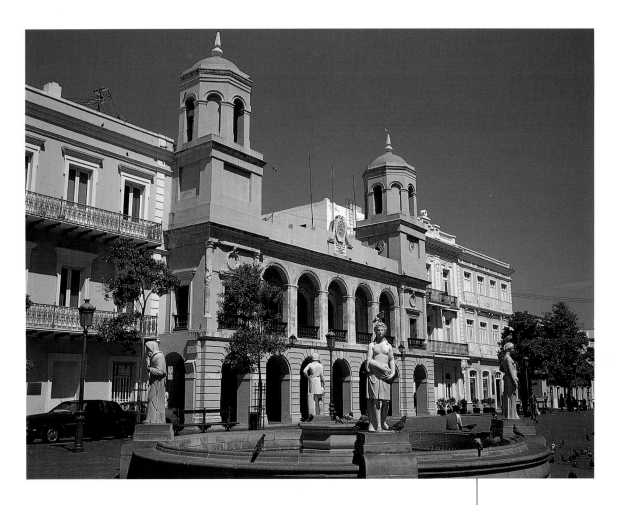

ARCHITECTURE

Four centuries of Spanish rule have left a legacy of beautiful Spanish colonial architecture in Puerto Rico. Examples of these are especially to be found in San Juan, Ponce, and other early Spanish settlements.

Many parts of San Juan, especially the old walled section built by the Spanish, still show the Spanish influence in Spanish-style architecture and narrow streets cobbled with blue-gray stones once used as ballast on Spanish sailing ships.

One aspect of Spanish buildings that fitted in with the Taíno settlements was that of a central square, which was important to both cultures. The *batey* or village square of the Taíno became the plazas under Spanish rule.

An example of Spanish colonial architecture in the Plaza de Armas in San Juan. Many old colonial buildings have been carefully restored by the Institute of Puerto Rican Culture.

95

LEISURE

LEISURE TIME IS TAKEN very seriously in Puerto Rico. Weekends are the most important time for people to unwind. Puerto Rican leisure activities range from spending a night out in the local town square chatting to playing dominoes and listening to impromptu music recitals in the streets.

Spectator sports such as baseball, horse racing, and cockfighting are very popular. A major tourist attraction is gambling, which takes place officially in casinos or unofficially over cockfights.

Music plays a large part in the daily life of the people, and the many festivals provide lots of fun fiesta time. Cinemas and libraries are not so popular as they are quiet and solitary activities, but weekend family picnics and trips to the country to visit farms are popular. For the wealthy and tourists, golf, water sports, and deep-sea fishing are all available, and Puerto Rico's beautiful beaches have their fair share of surfers.

Opposite: **A competitor and his horse at a** *paso fino* **horse competition.** *Paso fino* **horses are ponies or tiny horses originally brought from Spain. Their name means "delicate stride."**

Left: **Street concerts are a common sight, with both adults and children taking part.**

Volleyball players on Luquillo beach. Volleyball is a popular beach sport.

BASEBALL

The national sport of Puerto Rico is baseball. It was brought to Puerto Rico around the turn of the century by the Americans.

Puerto Rico takes part in the Caribbean League, which is played from October to March, and all the major cities have teams. There are games almost daily in Puerto Rico, and serious fans also watch the Atlanta Braves games on national television, as well as satellite coverage from the United States.

Many Puerto Rican players have been signed up by the American major leagues. As early as the 1940s, Hiram Bithorn played for Chicago and Louis Olmo played for the Brooklyn Dodgers. The greatest Puerto Rican baseball player of all was Roberto Clemente. Orlando Cepeda is another name familiar to baseball fans. He played with the San Francisco Giants from 1958. In 1965, after a serious knee injury, he spent a year out of the game but made an excellent comeback the following year with the St. Louis Cardinals. In 1967, he was voted the National League's most valuable player.

OTHER SPORTS

Basketball is another popular sport. It is largely an amateur sport with teams in most of the major cities that take part in the Central American and Caribbean Games.

Golf, swimming, and tennis are more exclusive sporting activities, mainly in luxury hotels. Puerto Rico has produced stars in all three fields. The most famous is Chi Chi Rodriguez, who started his career as a caddie and discovered a special talent for golf. He joined the Professional Golf Association tour in 1960, and in 25 years, he won eight tournaments and became a millionaire. In tennis, Charlito Passarell became a world class player during the 1970s.

ROBERTO CLEMENTE

Roberto Clemente showed his talent as a player from an early age. He played baseball with Santurce while still at school.

By the time he was 20, talent scouts from the United States came to watch him play, and he signed up with the Pittsburgh Pirates in 1955. In his 18 years with the team, he won many awards and honors including the Gold Glove award for outstanding fielding. He received this award 11 times.

But it was not just as a baseball player that Puerto Ricans remember Clemente. He was also devoted to his country and came up with the idea of developing a sports city for Puerto Rican children. He gave generously to charities and spent much of his time working for good causes. In December 1972, when he was flying to Nicaragua to do relief work at an earthquake site, his plane crashed and he was killed. He was 38.

Roberto Clemente was inducted into the Baseball Hall of Fame in 1973 and remains one of the few players ever to hit 3,000 base hits.

COCKFIGHTING

Banned in most parts of the world, cockfighting is a major leisure pursuit in Puerto Rico and a source of income for some. It takes place in *gallera* ("gah-YEH-rah") or galleries that are found all over the island.

The cocks are matched in pairs, and the bird that does the most damage is the winner. The birds wear spurs and fight on until one dies or flies out of the cockpit. Birds may have pedigrees similar to thoroughbred racehorses and are specially bred for the sport.

Hundreds of dollars change hands in an informal system of betting. Few of the profits from gambling are ever declared, and some people supplement low wages or welfare payments with their winnings. It is mainly a male working class sport, accompanied by drinking and shouting.

In boxing too, Puerto Rico has produced winners—in the 1930s, Sixto Escobar held the National Boxing Association's bantamweight title three times.

Surfing is a growing sport with the World Surfing Championships held on the island several times. Many of the best surfing areas are close to the capital and young Puerto Ricans enjoy this sport.

Horses have always been a major love of the Puerto Ricans, and betting on horse racing is a major pastime. There is one horse track in San Juan but people can bet at any of hundreds of offtrack betting parlors all around the island.

Horse riding is popular in the northwest of the island at Arenales, on Vieques Island, and at Coamo in the central mountains where the traditional *paso fino* ("pah-soh FEE-noh") horses are bred. Their delicate stride suits the difficult terrain of Puerto Rico, especially in the mountains. Herds of *paso fino* horses also run wild on Vieques Island. An annual *paso fino* show is held in Puerto Rico every year.

EVENING PURSUITS

In the warm evenings of Puerto Rico, an enjoyable activity is to sit in a street bar, coffee shop, or in the town square, chat with friends, and watch the world go by. Local *plena* groups perform on the streets on weekends, while young men and women eye one another. People also play cards and games out in the street. Dominoes and chess are very popular games.

Watching television is just as popular as in the United States. Programs are broadcast in Spanish and English, and Puerto Ricans are familiar with most modern American and Latin American soap operas.

Gambling at casinos on blackjack, roulette, and slot machines is largely for the wealthy and for tourists. Casinos are more formal than in the United States and people are required to be well dressed. A popular form of gambling is the weekly lottery, which provides an enormous income for the government. There are also less regulated local lotteries called *la bolita* ("lah boh-LEE-tah") with smaller stakes.

Men playing cards in the street in the cool of the evening.

VACATIONS

Puerto Rico is a very beautiful island with lots of unspoiled areas for recreation. For those who prefer to get back to nature, there are the nature reserves to visit or a trek through the central mountains.

Many people take driving vacations around the island, especially city dwellers who go back to the countryside to keep in touch with their rural roots. A popular drive is the 165 mile Panoramic Route, which follows the Cordillera Central through forest reserves and rural towns. It runs from the southeastern town of Yabucoa to Mayagüez on the west coast. On weekends, many families drive into the country for picnics. For those who live in the countryside, the city of San Juan provides the excitement of city life.

A popular holiday destination and resort for Puerto Rican families is the Coamo spa in the Cordillera Central, which has natural hot springs. The water is a constant 110° Fahrenheit.

Sailing and windsurfing at Ocean Park beach near San Juan. With their many public beaches, Puerto Ricans have all the ingredients of a sunny, lazy holiday right at their doorstep.

ANCIENT TAÍNO BALL GAMES

The Taíno Indians must also have been great sports fans if the remains of their ancient ball courts are anything to go by. Archeological remains of Taíno ball courts dating back to A.D. 1100 have been found in the Caguana Indian Ceremonial Park near the town of Utuado.

Large rectangular courts were marked out with stones, and remains of what are thought to be belt bats have been found. They are large stone rings that were worn around the hips and used to hit a ball from one side of the court to another. The teams lost points for letting the ball fall to the ground and gained them for scoring goals.

A 16th century account of such a game tells of players being carried off the field dead and others wounding their thighs and knees as they hit the ball to the other side of the court. In the ancient Mayan civilization of Mexico, a similar game is depicted on wall friezes. In these, the winning team was allowed to take all the jewelry of the audience, while the losing team was beheaded, so it must have been a very serious game indeed.

FESTIVALS

PUERTO RICO'S HOLIDAYS AND FESTIVALS are a year-round experience. Besides Puerto Rican holidays, the island also celebrates some American holidays, bringing the total public holidays to around 20. In addition, there are festivals organized by each town to mark its patron saint's day. Since each town has a different patron saint, that adds up to lots of festivals.

Many Puerto Rican festivals have become tourist attractions and a grand excuse for street parties, with fairgrounds, gambling, and lots of music.

PUERTO RICAN HOLIDAYS

January 1	New Year's Day
January 6	Three Kings' Day
January 11	De Hostos' Birthday
January 15	Martin Luther King Jr. Day
January 22	Washington's Birthday
March 11	Emancipation Day
April	Good Friday, Easter
April 16	José de Diego's Birthday
May 30	Memorial Day
July 4	Independence Day
July 17	Muñoz Rivera's Birthday
July 25	Constitution Day
July 27	Celsos Barbosa's Birthday
September 1	Labor Day
September 23	Grito de Lares
October 12	Columbus Day
November 11	Veterans Day
November 19	Discovery of Puerto Rico Day
November	Thanksgiving
December 25	Christmas

Opposite: **Festivals and street processions are an occasion for people to dress up. Here they dress up as Ferdinand and Isabella, king and queen of Spain during the time of Christopher Columbus.**

Among the American holidays celebrated in Puerto Rico are Washington's Birthday, Martin Luther King Jr. Day, Independence Day, and Thanksgiving.

PUBLIC HOLIDAYS

Many Puerto Rican holidays commemorate historical events and celebrate the birthdays of important citizens. January 11 is the birthday of Eugenio María de Hostos, who supported the abolition of slavery and independence from Spain. He was exiled from Puerto Rico for his political beliefs and spent several years living in the Dominican Republic.

March 11 commemorates the abolition of slavery in Puerto Rico. April 16 celebrates the birthday of José de Diego, who was secretary of justice in the few weeks of independence before the Spanish-American War. He became president of the House of Representatives under United States rule and spent his political life campaigning for independence.

July 17 is the birthday of Luis Muñoz Rivera, who negotiated autonomy with Spain and later became Puerto Rico's commissioner to the United States. Constitution Day on July 25 commemorates Puerto Rico's commonwealth status in 1952, and also marks the day on which the U.S. invasion of the island began.

July 27 marks the birthday of the founder of the Puerto Rican Republican party, Dr. José Celso Barbosa, in 1857. September 23 is the anniversary of Grito de Lares, when independence was first declared by rebels in Lares. Although the revolt was unsuccessful, it stands out as a time when Puerto Ricans began to fight for their independence. It was made a public holiday in 1968, the centennial of the event. Discovery Day on November 19 celebrates Christopher Columbus' arrival on the island.

Children play a big role in celebrating Puerto Rico's national day, taking part in parades and processions.

LAS NAVIDADES

The most important religious festival is Christmas or Las Navidades, which begins around St. Nicholas Day on December 15, and extends up to Three Kings' Day on January 6.

The Christmas season coincides with the beginning of the tourist season, so the island fills with foreign and Puerto Rican visitors. This is a time for family visits and parties, as families have several reunions, especially between Christmas and Three Kings' Day. Christmas Day celebrations begin with midnight mass when thousands of people flock to the churches. Even people who hardly attend church go to midnight mass.

Christmas Day is celebrated with a feast of traditional *léchon asado* ("leh-CHON ah-SAH-doh" or roast suckling pig,), *yuca*, chicken, rice, and pigeon peas. Lots of rum is drunk and a special concoction called *coquito* ("coh-CHEE-toh"), a mixture of rum and coconut milk.

Families sing carols together and observe the 19th century tradition of *asaltos* ("ah-ZAHL-tohs"). This tradition involves making surprise visits—groups of friends go from one house to another, calling to their friends to join the party. It is a very noisy procession with long stops for welcoming drinks at each house before the party moves on again. The party sings carols or *villancicos* ("vee-YAN-see-kohs") as it moves around. Children also go around the neighborhood singing carols, beating time with improvised percussion instruments, and asking for *aguinaldo* ("ah-gwee-NAHL-doh") or a small gift.

Easter is also an important religious holiday in Puerto Rico. Every Easter, a statue of the Virgin Mary is carried in a procession around San Juan.

107

A street band entertaining passers-by at the Fiesta Calle San Sebastian in San Juan.

The traditional time for giving gifts is Three Kings' Day on January 6, which is another official public holiday. On the eve of Three Kings' Day, children fill small boxes with grass for the kings' horses and Puerto Rican parents replace the grass with the children's gifts. It is also customary for parents to exchange gifts with people with whom they have a *compadrazgo* relationship.

SAINTS' FESTIVALS

While the formal religious events such as Christmas and Easter are solemn affairs, saints' festivals are celebrated in a more high-spirited way. Street parties, processions, huge dances in the town's central plaza, traveling fairs, lots of alcohol, gambling, and music are typical of saints' festivals. Since each town is associated with a particular saint, saints' festivals take place all year round in Puerto Rico.

FEAST OF SAN JUAN BAUTISTA This is the most important saint's day in Puerto Rico. For days before, parties, carnivals, and dances are held in town squares. On the afternoon of June 23, all business in San Juan comes to a halt and thousands of families head to the beach. The rest of the day is a beach party, where *salsa* music is played and food is barbequed all night. At midnight, people observe the tradition of walking backward into the sea to greet St. John the Baptist, patron saint of Puerto Rico.

NUESTRA SENORA DE LA MONSERRATE While most of the saints' festivals in Puerto Rico have taken on the atmosphere of a major party, this one has retained much of its religious significance.

In the small town of Hormigueros in the southwest of Puerto Rico, there is a magnificent Cathedral of Our Lady of Monserrat. In September each year, pilgrims come to the town to celebrate the saint's festival and do penance by climbing the stone stairs of the cathedral on their knees.

Young people on the steps of a church on Palm Sunday. Some are dressed in clothes from biblical times.

Bonfires are lit on Candeleria Day on February 2. Every family in the community brings a piece of wood to the bonfire to protect their house from burning down for the next year.

109

FEAST OF SANTIAGO APOSTOL One of the most famous saints' festivals in Puerto Rico is celebrated in Loíza. The festival marks the saint's day of St. James the Apostle and lasts for a week beginning July 25.

The opening of the festival is marked by a procession in which ceremonial costumes and masks are worn. As this festival is held in a town with a large African population, these costumes are remarkably similar to those still used by the Yoruba tribe in Nigeria. Although the festival is a Spanish one, many of the details are African.

The Christian tradition behind the costumes and masks is to make people scared of hell and to draw them back to the church. The masks are carved from coconut shells and painted in bright colors. They are given the appearance of scary faces with long sharp teeth and devil's horns. The masks are worn by young men called *veigantes* whose job it once was to scare lapsed Christians back to church. Other participants in the parade are *viejos* ("vee-EH-hohs" or old men), masqueraders, and *bomba* dancers accompanied by the *bomba* drum made from a wooden barrel.

The dancing is fast and rhythmic like African dances. Figures of the saints are carried in the processions. Special masses are also said in church. The usual traveling sideshows and fairground rides, small gambling games, and lots of drinking exist side by side with the religious element of the festival.

FESTIVAL OF OUR LADY OF GUADALUPE This saint's festival is celebrated in February by the people of Ponce, Puerto Rico's second oldest city. It also draws on the tradition of masked figures scaring the unholy back to the church. Ponce masqueraders wear masks that are made of gourds and have a distinctive style. The Ponce festival is similar to the Loíza festival, especially since the African influence is also seen in the costumes and music of the festival.

A wall mural commemorating the festival of Santiago Apostol shows the Spanish and African traditions in this festival. While a Spanish soldier waves his sword, figures wearing African-style masks and costumes form part of a procession.

A modern festival organized by the tourist board is the Le Lo Lai festival. It aims to show what Puerto Rican festivals are like to tourists who do not get a chance to see an actual saints' festival.

THE PABLO CASALS FESTIVAL

This festival began in 1957 when the famous cellist, Pablo Casals, whose mother was Puerto Rican, adopted the island as his home. He established a festival of classical music, which has since become the greatest cultural and musical event in the Caribbean, with people coming from all over the world to perform.

The festival is held in May each year and attracts many famous composers who are happy to have their work premiered in San Juan by the Puerto Rico Symphony Orchestra.

A coffee festival in one of the small towns draws many people from rural areas.

FOOD

PUERTO RICAN FOOD IS A MIXTURE of Spanish, native Indian, and African food and cooking styles. Before the Spanish settlers came, native vegetables were sweet potatoes, cassava, yams, peanuts, a kind of chili, tobacco, and corn. The Spanish brought cash crops, vegetables, and meat from all over the Spanish empire. Many of the modern crops, such as coffee, coconuts, sugarcane, bananas, and oranges, were introduced by the Spanish. Plantains, potatoes, and onions supplemented the local root vegetables. The meat of sheep, cattle, pigs, hens, and goats was added to the diet of those who could afford it.

The taste of all these was also given a boost by the arrival of ginger, garlic, tomatoes, and many previously unknown spices such as coriander, cumin, and some newer forms of chili. The Puerto Ricans used all these new spices to develop a distinctive style of cooking, unlike Latin American, Spanish, Taíno, or African cooking. Although American fast foods are available in Puerto Rico, the ethnic style of cooking is still very popular.

TAÍNO FOODS

Native Taíno food staples were corn, cassava, sweet potatoes, yams, peanuts, and some other starchy roots. Their supply of meat was limited to birds that they caught, iguanas, local guinea pigs, oysters, clams, turtles, and other seafood. Although there are no original Taíno people left in Puerto Rico, their influence on the local food can still be seen.

Opposite: **Being an island, Puerto Rico has a wide selection of fish and seafood.**

Above: **Bottles of hot chili sauce for sale at roadside stalls.**

113

A re-creation of Taíno cooking methods. The Taíno used cooking and eating utensils made from the gourds of the calabash tree.

Fresh fruit is plentiful in Puerto Rico, although most of the fruits are unfamiliar to Americans. A fruit called the custard apple in English has a creamy custard-tasting flesh. The *quenepa* ("koo-eh-NEH-pah"), or Spanish lime, is a walnut-sized fruit with a hard skin that reveals a pink, citrus-tasting flesh when peeled. Other fruits are the hog plum and genipap.

The Taíno also made a kind of bread out of mashed cassava root mixed with water and baked between two stones. One Taíno drink that was consumed at religious festivals was a tea made from the flowers of the *campaña* ("cahm-PAH-nyah") tree, which had a hallucinogenic effect.

MEALTIMES

Surprisingly, the Spanish tradition of a big lunch followed by a *siesta* ("see-EHS-tah") is not so common. In Puerto Rico, eating habits depend on the working day. In the hotter and drier parts of the island and in country areas where agriculture is the main activity, people have long lunches followed by a *siesta*.

But in towns and industrial areas, people have just an hour's lunch break with no *siesta*. For most city people, lunch is a sandwich or rice and beans in one of the local *fondas* ("FOHN–dahs"), or roadside stalls. The main evening meal with the family is more elaborate, but this also depends on whether both parents work.

Roadside food stalls or *fondas* and restaurants cater to the lunch crowd.

Roadside stalls offer a variety of dishes. Customers can take their pick of dishes to eat with rice or beans.

TYPICAL PUERTO RICAN MEALS

Breakfast in cities tends to be boiled or fried eggs and coffee. In the countryside, the traditional breakfast is ground cereal mixed with hot milk.

The midday meal and the evening meal have more traditional foods, especially rice and beans, which are the staple foods. The legumes commonly grown and eaten are white beans, kidney beans, garbanzo beans, and pigeon peas. These are all regular elements of the main meals of the day. The most typical way of cooking beans is in a *sofrito* ("soh-FREE-toh") sauce made from bacon or ham, tomatoes, garlic, chilies, coriander, and other spices. The beans and sauce are poured over rice and eaten.

Two other important staple foods in Puerto Rico are plantain and bananas. Unripe plantain is sliced and fried to become crisp *tostones* ("tohs-TOH-nehs"), which are served with rice and *sofrito* sauce, or with meat stews. Ripe yellow plantains and green bananas are boiled and served as vegetables.

Meat is still a luxury for poorer families and is not eaten every day. Pork is made into a variety of dishes. Besides chops and legs of pork, there is *cuchifrito* ("cooh-chih-FREE-toh," a stew of internal organs), *mondongo* ("mohn-DOHNG-goh," or pork tripe cut into small pieces and stewed in *sofrito* sauce), and *gandinga* ("gahn-DING-gah," which is stewed pork liver, heart, and kidneys mixed with vegetables). These are served with rice.

The most famous pork dish is the *léchon asado*, which is served at Christmas. It is spit-roasted until the skin is dry and crisp. A delicacy called *chicharrón* ("chih-chahr-ON") uses large chunks of pork skin as a plate on which meat, rice, and sauce are poured. After eating the meat and rice, people eat up the edible pork-skin plate.

Chicken is cooked many ways but one particular specialty is *asopao* ("ah-soh-pow"), a stew made with chicken and rice.

Beef is regularly eaten in a Puerto Rican form of steak, but cut thinner and with a slightly tougher texture. A special beef dish is *carne mechada* ("CAR-neh meh-CHAH-dah"), a beef roast stuffed with spices and onion. Beef is also one of the main ingredients of *piononos* ("pee-oh-NOH-nohs") or stuffed plantains. A sauce similar to *sofrito* is added to the fried ground beef, sandwiched in fried plantain slices, and then deep-fried. Another beef dish is cooked *al caldero* ("ahl cahl-DEH-roh"), that is, in the traditional Puerto Rican cooking pot, a cauldron with a tightly-fitted lid.

Fish is less commonly eaten than beef and pork, but one fish staple is salted dried codfish. This is a prime ingredient of a dish served during Lent—*serenata* ("zehr-eh-NAH-tah"), which is cooked in vinaigrette sauce and served with a salad of tomatoes, avocados, and onions.

Puerto Rico also has snack foods such as fritters of various meats or codfish cooked in hot oil, or *pastelillos* ("pahs-tell-YEEL-johs"), or little pies made from plantains filled with fried meats, cheese, or even jam.

Desserts are often based on locally grown coconuts. *Flan de coco* ("flan deh COH-coh") is a custard made from coconuts and eggs blended with caramelized sugar. Coconut is also used in *bienmesabe* ("bee-en-meh-SAH-

Puerto Rican cooking uses a wide range of spices and herbs. The African influence can be seen in the way the different foods are blended to make unusual textures and tastes.

beh") sauce, a syrup made from coconut milk, sugar, and egg yolks. It is poured over sponge cake fingers, or ladyfingers, or even okra and eaten. A soft cheese made in Puerto Rico is served with fruit, as a dessert.

PUERTO RICAN KITCHENS

In San Juan and other towns, modern kitchens have electrical gadgets and microwave ovens for heating up dinners. But in the countryside, things are a little more in keeping with the old ways of doing things.

The main feature of traditional Puerto Rican kitchens was the *caldera,* a large round cast-iron cooking pot with a tight-fitting lid that was used for cooking over a wood-burning stove. This cooking pot is native only to Puerto Rico and was used to cook dishes such as stews quite slowly, or as an oven to dry-roast meat.

Many Puerto Rican kitchens in homes with a garden have herb and spice gardens just outside the door. Most foods are bought fresh from the local market. Fruits and vegetables from local farms are easily available, as well as the local soft white cheese made from cow's milk. Supermarkets sell an increasing number of processed American foods, but these are expensive and are rare in country kitchens.

A PUERTO RICAN RECIPE: *SURILLITOS*

An easy recipe to try in order to appreciate the flavor of Puerto Rican cooking is *surillitos* ("sooh-reh-JEE-tohs"). These are cheese and cornmeal fritters that are very popular snacks. They can also be served as bread with meals. They are best eaten while still hot and make a nice accompaniment to spicy stews.

Ingredients
$^3/_4$ pint water
1 teaspoon salt
6 oz yellow cornmeal
4 oz grated Edam or cheddar cheese
lard or cooking oil for frying

Boil water in a saucepan and add salt. Add the cornmeal, pouring it in a steady stream and stirring all the time to avoid lumps forming.

Cook for about 5 minutes over a gentle heat until the mixture is thick and smooth. Turn off the heat and add the grated cheese. Allow to cool.

Heat the lard or cooking oil in a large frying pan. Shape the cooled batter into cigar-shaped cylinders about 3 inches long and 1 inch wide.

Fry the cornsticks two at a time until they are evenly browned. Serve while still warm.

The famous Pina Colada cocktail is made from rum.

RUM

The development of the sugar industry resulted in the production of rum, one of Puerto Rico's more important industries.

Sugar production results in a by-product called molasses, a dark brown liquid. Besides being useful in animal feed, when molasses comes into contact with yeast, it begins to ferment. The yeast reacts with molasses to produce alcohol. This was first made into a wine called *aguardiente* ("ah-goo-are-dee-EN-teh") and was widely drunk in the early years of Spanish rule.

To produce rum, the wine is distilled to evaporate most of the water content and clear out any impurities. Nowadays, rum is made in computerized plants with carefully controlled yeast strains added to the molasses. This mixture is left to ferment in the first stage of the process that produces the wine, which is then put into a huge still to drive off the excess water. The alcohol obtained is very strong.

From this storage and treatment process, white, silver, or gold rum is produced. Gold rum has more molasses in it but has artificial coloring. White rum is filtered to take out the taste of the molasses.

Many popular cocktails use rum as their base. Daiquiris are made from gold rum mixed with sweet lime juice and crushed ice, and the Cuba Libre cocktail is white rum mixed with a cola drink. Another pleasant drink made from rum is hot rum toddy, where lemon, spices, and hot water are added to gold rum.

COFFEE

Coffee is now a less important crop in Puerto Rico because the costs of production have risen so much. But it is still grown on the lower slopes of some mountains where the good drainage suits the plants.

In the late 19th century, Puerto Rican grown coffee, called Yauco coffee after the place where it was grown, was considered among the best in the world. Whether it is due to the strain of plant, the climate, or the treatment of the plant, Puerto Rican coffee is stronger than typical American coffee.

Coffee is drunk during the day *con leche* ("con LEH-cheh")—with a half portion of milk and another half portion of very strong coffee. After dinner in the evening, it is drunk demitasse—in a tiny cup, and black with sugar. Coffee is served in tiny paper cups all over the island at small roadside stalls, more as a stimulant than as a thirst quencher.

Ice-cream seller in old San Juan.

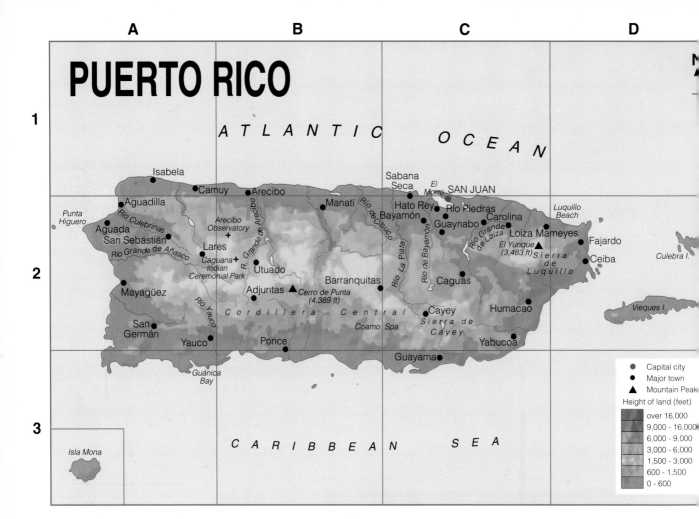

PUERTO RICO

QUICK NOTES

OFFICIAL NAME
The Commonwealth of Puerto Rico

LAND AREA
3,435 square miles

POPULATION
3.6 million

CAPITAL
San Juan

MAJOR TOWNS
San Juan, Ponce, Mayagüez, Bayamón, Arecibo, Fajardo, Caguas, Aguadilla

HIGHEST POINT
Cerro de Punta (4,389 feet)

MAJOR RIVERS
Río La Plata, Río Grande de Loíza

NATIONAL ANTHEM
La Borinquéna

NATIONAL FLAG
Five horizontal stripes of red and white with a blue triangle on the left. Inside the triangle is a five-pointed white star.

OFFICIAL LANGUAGE
Spanish

MAJOR RELIGION
Roman Catholicism

CURRENCY
US dollar

MAIN EXPORTS
Pharmaceuticals, electronics, rum, sugar, tobacco, coffee

IMPORTANT ANNIVERSARIES
Emancipation Day, March 11
Muñoz Rivera's Birthday, July 17
Constitution Day, July 25
Grito de Lares Day, September 23
Discovery of Puerto Rico Day,
  November 19

POLITICAL LEADERS
Luis Muñoz Rivera (1829–1916), negotiated
  Charter of Autonomy with Spain, com-
  missioner to Washington.
Luis Muñoz Marín (1898–1980), governor
  from 1948 to 1964.
Luis A. Ferré, governor from 1968 to 1972.
Rafael Hernández Colón, governor from
  1984 to 1992.

GLOSSARY

barrio ("BAH-ree-oh") Local area or neighborhood.

batey ("BAH-tey") The central square of Taíno villages.

Boriquén ("boh-ree-KANE") The Taíno Indian name for Puerto Rico.

caldera ("cahl-DEH-rah") Traditional large cooking pot with rounded bottom and a tightly-fitting lid.

compadrazgo ("cohm-pahd-RAZ-goh") Relationship between close friends, similar to that of godparents.

compadre ("cohm-PAH-dreh") Godfather to a child or a close family friend.

jíbaro ("HEE-bah-row") Puerto Rican peasant farmer.

Jurakan ("hoo-rah-KAHN") Taíno name for the devil from which the English word "hurricane" is derived.

karst The effect of weathering on limestone rock creating sinkholes and underground passages.

machismo ("mah-KHIZ-moh") Latin belief that men are superior to women.

patrón ("pah-TRON") Local or neighborhood landlord in rural areas.

plena ("PLAY-nyah") An improvised musical piece played on percussion instruments.

salsa ("SAHL-zah") African-style music that uses drums.

Taíno Native Indians that inhabited Puerto Rico before the Spanish arrival.

yuca ("YOO-kah") Cassava. One of the traditional foods of the Taíno and a common vegetable in Puerto Rican food today.

BIBLIOGRAPHY

Jerome J. Aliotta: *The Puerto Ricans*, Chelsea House, New York, 1991.

Arturo Morales Carrión: *Puerto Rico: A Political and Cultural History*, Norton, New York, 1983.

Olga Jiminez de Wagenheim: *Puerto Rico's Revolt for Independence*, Westview Press, Boulder, Colorado, 1985.

Clifford A. Hauberg: *Puerto Rico and Puerto Ricans*, Twayne, New York, 1974.

Insight Guides: *Puerto Rico*, APA Publications, Hong Kong, 1987.

Harry S. Pariser: *The Adventure Guide to Puerto Rico*, Hunter Publishing, New Jersey, 1989.

Clara Rodriguez: *Puerto Ricans: Born in the USA*, Unwin Hyman, Boston, 1989.

Karl Wagenheim: *Puerto Rico: A Profile*, Praeger, New York, 1970.

INDEX

INDEX

INDEX

PICTURE CREDITS
Douglas Donne Bryant Stock Photography: 3, 5, 9, 12, 15, 23, 24, 28, 29, 44, 45, 47, 49, 50, 51, 54, 55, 56, 58, 59, 60, 73, 86, 88, 89, 90, 91, 93, 96, 97, 102, 103, 104, 107, 108, 109, 111, 113, 114, 118
The Image Bank: 38, 42, 71
International Photobank: 14, 18, 21, 64, 70, 100
Björn Klingwall: 10, 31, 33, 40, 43
Life File Photo Library: 11, 34, 35, 75, 95, 101, 120, 121, 123
David Simson: 1, 4, 6, 7, 17 (both), 30, 46, 48, 52, 53, 62, 65, 67, 68, 69, 72, 77, 78, 80, 82, 83, 84, 85, 87, 98, 106, 110, 112, 115, 116, 117